STRAWBERRY KISS

The Benningtons
Book 2

ANNABELLE MARIN

Published by Blushing Books
An Imprint of
ABCD Graphics and Design, Inc.
A Virginia Corporation
977 Seminole Trail #233
Charlottesville, VA 22901

Strawberry Kiss
Annabelle Marin

EBook ISBN: 978-1-63954-476-9
Print ISBN: 978-1-63954-477-6

The Bennington Family Tree

- Petunia Bennington (1822-1859)
- Paul Bennington (1821-1870)
- Christopher Bennington (b.1840. 31 years old)
- Lucille "Lucy" Bennington (nee Robbins) (b.1847. 24 years old)
- Steve Bennington (b.1842. 29 years old)
- Hugh Bennington (b.1845. 26 years old)
- Poppy Bennington (b.1845. 26 years old)
- Anthony Bennington (b.1849. 22 years old)
- Iris Bennington (b.1855. 16 years old)
- Lily Bennington (b.1859. 12 years old)

Chapter 1

AUGUST 1870, *Larkspur Valley, Wyoming...*

Eighteen-year-old Ruby Green wanted to beat someone to a bloody pulp. Or at the very least, she wanted to scratch their eyeballs out. It was the perfect way to describe her irritation. She had been stuck in the stupid stagecoach, going from her own worthless little town full of poverty, shady characters, and murderers, to the much larger and dignified Larkspur Valley which boasted about their good, Christian spirit.

She was hungry, had less than five dollars to her name, and her best dress of blue and white calico was a dirty mess which clung to her sweaty, half-starved body. In short, she had more than enough reasons to be an irritated mess.

She should be wearing black, as her father had died from drinking too much and was buried only a week ago, but she didn't have enough clothes. Besides, her father had never been someone to mourn over.

It will all be worth it, Ruby, just you watch, she told herself as she forced her way out of the stagecoach. She held a brown, worn-out satchel, which her father had used when he had gone to school as a young man before he became the town drunk and married her whore mother.

"She was beautiful, your mother," he would often blubber when the alcohol would start settling in his stomach. Thankfully, her father was never a violent drunk. At most, he would just force her to dance or sing before sleeping the rest of the afternoon off. "Looked like an angel. Sang like one too. You, my Ruby, are the spitting image of her."

Ruby never knew if her father was telling the truth or if he was confusing her mother for someone else. Her mother had died when Ruby was only two, strangled by the hands of one of her clients when he had refused to pay for enjoying her body. The client had gotten off scot-free because he had been the sheriff's brother-in-law, but her poor mother had to be buried in a shallow grave off the beaten path because the church would not accept a whore being buried in their graveyard.

But she imagined there must be some truth to her father's statement because he hadn't been the only one who had commented on her looks. Ruby was a stunning blonde who loved letting her pale locks fly free across her shoulders, even if women often rudely commented the type of hairstyle was only appropriate on young girls, not someone who was on the verge of womanhood.

Her green eyes had often been described as catlike, with her tongue equally sharp and ready to insult anyone she fancied. An array of light freckles adorned the top of her cheeks and nose which she often tried to cover with rouge.

Ruby Green knew she was a beautiful girl.

She was hopeful her beauty would make her a rich girl.

Before her mother had been murdered, she had been an "independent" whore who didn't belong to a brothel and entertained men in her own home. Her father often boasted about how her mother had earned money, jewels, and expensive presents as she charmed men with her beauty.

But unlike her mother, she would not be killed, and unlike her father, she would not spend it all on alcohol and stale peanuts. Ruby reached into the pocket of her dress and pulled out an old watch which had belonged to her father.

It was almost five in the evening, which meant she had to reach the brothel before it became busy for the evening. Starting off in a brothel, was not her first choice, but despite her less than stellar homelife, she was still hopelessly naive about the "pleasures of the flesh". Ruby thought it would be for the best if she started in a traditional brothel, to learn the tricks of the trade before she went on her own way.

A year would be enough to learn how to pleasure a man and she would be able to save money on room and board.

Her green eyes scanned Larkspur Valley. This town was so big, much bigger than the town she had come from, where a person could visit every single spot in less than twenty minutes. This town felt like it went on forever. If Ruby was still a childish fool, she would have compared it to something out of a storybook.

She bit her lower lip. The brothel must be on the outskirts of town, away from the big, white church, so it must mean—

"Are you lost, little lady? Where's your daddy?"

The voice was condescending with a hint of teasing, as if Ruby were a little girl and not a grown woman. She turned around to give the bastard a piece of her mind.

The first thing she saw was a large, gold sheriff's badge attached to a clean, stiff brown vest. A brown cowboy hat sat on top of black, inky curls. The man was smiling, showing off a row of white teeth. His blue eyes were the same shade as the sky—the kind of eyes baby angels had.

He was handsome, but being handsome did not take

away his rudeness, especially at a time when she didn't want to be bothered. So, this giant with the sunny blue eyes was the town sheriff. She wondered if he could throw a decent punch. He seemed like too much of a pretty boy, even though his arms were thicker than her neck.

"My father is dead," she replied coldly.

The sheriff had the decency to look embarrassed as he removed his hat. "I'm sorry for your loss. I apologize for my tasteless joke. I'm Sheriff Steve Bennington. Is there anything I can help you with, Miss—"

Finally, someone in this town was making themselves useful.

Ruby offered her pale hand towards him so he could kiss it. "Ruby Green. Yes, you can help me. I need you to tell me where the brothel is. No need to walk me to it, you can just point me to it."

Sheriff Bennington looked beyond horrified, as if she had just told him she ate rattlesnakes for breakfast. It was quite amusing. "A brothel?" he inquired politely. "Is that truly the place you want to go to, Miss Green? It is not a good place for impressionable young ladies. If you need a place to stay, I can point you in the direction of the nearest inn."

"It won't be necessary, Sheriff Bennington. Now, the directions for the brothel if you please, or do I have to ask someone else?" she asked sweetly.

Sheriff Bennington narrowed his eyes, obviously thinking she was making fun of him. She didn't know why. Ruby knew she certainly didn't look the part of a respectable young lady with her tangled hair and dirty clothes.

"It's three blocks down, Larkspur Heaven, next to the saloon in front of the feed store. Madame Eugenia owns it. You can't miss it," he said slowly, his eyes never leaving hers.

So, this town's brothel wasn't in the middle of nowhere. It would certainly make everything much easier for her. Ruby gave a small curtsy in a mocking way, as if he were a member of the aristocracy. "Thank you."

Ruby could feel his eyes peering at the back of her head as she made her way to the brothel with the tacky name of Larkspur Heaven. The whorehouse seemed as old and unkempt as the saloon next door, painted a faded green with ugly, brown shutters and creaky windows and doors. A worn-out yellow sign with a crooked, painted larkspur flower read, *Larkspur Heaven.*

There was a bit of a commotion happening as the workers got ready for the evening rush. Women gossiped as they brushed their hair and people watched from the upstairs rooms. Three older women plumped up couch cushions outside while they complained about how dusty they were. A tall, bald man with a thick mustache looked around carefully as if he expected an attack at any moment. He was a guard of some sort and the only one who would be able to get her a front row seat to see Madame Eugenia.

Ruby arched her back and started walking towards the entrance like a young queen. The bald man stepped in front of the door almost immediately. "Who are you?" he spat.

Ruby gave him her most patient smile. "I'm Ruby Green. I was hoping to speak to Madame Eugenia."

"She's not interested in anything you have to sell, girl."

"Oh, but I'm not selling anything, sir. You see, I am interested in working for Madame Eugenia as a lady of the night, to put it politely."

She regretted her words as soon as she said them. Why did she dance around the subject? She should have said "whore". Now, he would think she was an ignorant fool.

The man narrowed his eyes. "You? Working upstairs, spreading those pale white legs of yours and accepting every miner, farmer, rancher, and storekeeper who stores a coin in your bosom?"

Ruby hoped she wasn't blushing even though she felt her skin turning hot. "Correct. Now, may I please speak with her? I've been traveling all day."

He looked like he wanted to slap her but, eventually, led her inside. The place smelled of soap and strong perfume, nicer than she had anticipated. The brothel was so busy with workers arranging card tables and getting plates and beer glasses ready, they didn't pay attention to Ruby at all.

"Follow me," the bald man ordered.

He took her to a small office at the back, behind the staircase, covered head to toe in red velvet with a fancy-looking chandelier. A plump woman was sitting at the desk in the back, her large breasts nearly popping out of her tightly corseted dress. There was a large emerald and pearl choker around her thick neck. Deep red rouge covered her cheeks, and her overly thin eyebrows rose in surprise when she looked at Ruby.

"Frank, what is this?"

"I'm Ruby Green," Ruby butted in before the bald man could answer, ignoring the sting at being referred to as an object. "I want a job here as a prostitute, to sleep with men." There, that sounded natural enough. She might have grown up with a drunk father and a whore mother, but deep down, she was like an innocent, pathetic schoolgirl.

Madame Eugenia and Frank exchanged looks before they burst out laughing at her naivety.

"Is there any other work a prostitute does?" The woman lit a thick cigar. "What's your name again, girl?"

She raised her chin proudly. "Ruby Green."

"How old are you, Ruby?"

"Eighteen."

"Have you ever fucked a man? Sucked him off? Bent down on all fours with your ass in the air, being offered like a platter?"

With every question, her face grew redder as she struggled with an answer.

Madame Eugenia let out a puff of air. "Get out of here, girl, and get a decent job as a seamstress or a kitchen maid at a hotel."

"It won't get me the money I want. Those jobs don't pay well. You work like a dog for every penny. Here, you earn twice the money with a single roll in the hay. I don't care about being a respectable woman if that's what you're wondering."

They exchanged looks before Frank spoke up. "We could give her a try. The men always become crazy dogs for virgins."

"I do hope you know what you're doing, girl. Your reputation will never be safe after entering this place." Madame Eugenia peered at her. "When do you turn nineteen?"

"On January first."

"Only a few months from now. Good. You will work as a barmaid until then. Earn your keep and learn from the other girls."

"What? Why?" she spat furiously.

"Because, despite your age, you are still wet behind the ears. Not to mention, you have a horrible temper which needs taming. You need to know what you're getting yourself into before you make a rash decision. I don't do this with everyone. You should be kissing my feet in gratitude." Madame Eugenia seemed to take pleasure in looking at her sullen face. "What do you say, beautiful Ruby?"

"Fine!" Ruby agreed after a while, still looking displeased. "I assume room and board and food will be covered."

Madame Eugenia and Frank exchanged looks. "My, aren't you a greedy little beggar. I should have Frank wash your mouth with soap. Yes, room and board and food will be included. I will take fifty cents for every dollar you make. You are responsible for your own clothes. I do not want to hear any lip about men constantly ripping your clothes. It comes with the territory." She squeezed Frank's arm. "Frank is my security and my husband. What he says goes, understand?"

She nodded, not wanting to argue about how half of her earnings would go to Madame Eugenia. "When can I start?"

"Tomorrow. You look rather worse for wear today. We need to make you pretty. The other girls can lend you things while you earn money." Madame Eugenia snapped her fingers. "Go find Linda. She will take you to your room and lend you clothes. This is a brothel, so there is no sense in looking like a church girl."

Both she and Frank snickered as Ruby left the room, heading outside to find Linda. Ruby had been too busy looking around, she hardly noticed when she ran into a wall of muscle. She winced as she rubbed her forehead.

A pair of strong arms was holding her steady by her shoulders. "Sorry."

A wave of irritation crossed her body. Oh, no, not him again. The sheriff was looking at her with a disapproving frown on his face. She hadn't realized how big he was until they were standing close to each other.

She pulled back when she realized her breasts were practically rubbing against his vest. "Are you really doing this?" Sheriff Steve Bennington looked disapproving.

"Yes." Ruby raised her chin. "Not that it's any of your business."

"On the contrary, I'm the sheriff of this fine town. Everything each citizen does is my business."

"Are you worried about every particular citizen, Sheriff, or am I just a special case?"

"Look, girl, I doubt your folks will be too happy knowing what you're doing. I know times are tough, but working in a brothel is not something your pa or ma would approve of."

"My parents are dead, Sheriff, as I told you." She smiled coldly. "Pa drank himself to death and I'll be entertaining men just like my dear ol' ma. It's practically a family tradition at this point."

Steve glared at her, obviously not pleased with her sarcasm.

"There are other jobs, sweetheart." Steve's voice was almost gentle, filled with pity. The kind of pity Ruby hated. "I could help you find one. Lord, you're barely out of the schoolhouse. Opening your legs to strangers, is not the way to make a living. You're too—"

"Stupid? Headstrong? Naive?"

"Innocent," Steve interrupted, obviously annoyed by her interruption. He gripped her wrist. Why was this man being so annoying? It was exhausting. "Let me help you, Ruby. My older brother and my sister-in-law will know what to do. I even have a place where you could stay with my sisters."

Ruby managed to pull away from his iron grip, nearly falling on her bottom. "And I told you I don't need help. This is what I decided from the beginning, Sheriff Bennington. If you were a true gentleman like you claim to be, you would respect my decision and let me be."

Her stubbornness was starting to make him angry. She could tell just by the way his blue eyes were narrowing at her, like he wanted to strangle her.

Steve took a step forward, looking like he wanted to place her over his shoulder and carry her away from the brothel.

But Ruby was tiny; she managed to escape him, hiding behind Frank who had sneaked in front of her, like a cat. Frank promptly closed the door in his face.

"Sorry, we're closed."

Chapter 2

"YOU'RE THE NEW GIRL, which means you get the smallest room." Linda was walking at a brisk pace as if someone were chasing her, which meant Ruby had to raise her skirts, practically running to keep up with her. "The more clients you have, the more money you make, and the more money you make, the happier Madame Eugenia becomes. Maybe in the future, you'll have a bigger room. Talia has the nicest room right now; it even has a large window which overlooks the valley."

Linda's voice was filled with jealousy which made Ruby guess she probably wasn't as popular as Talia.

Thank you for the beauty, Mother, Ruby thought smugly as she made her way inside her new bedroom which was no bigger than a broom closet. It only had a thin mattress and a cracked pitcher and basin on top of a small table.

There were already two other girls talking about the previous night in loud whispers. One of the girls was tall, with broad shoulders and obvious padding under her dress to hide her boyish figure. The other one was short and plump, with big brown eyes and curly, dirty-blonde hair.

"New girl," Linda announced in a bored tone, as if Ruby were an annoying package. "Girls, this is Ruby Green. She's a barmaid for now but will be starting upstairs in January. Ruby, this is Estella," she pointed to the tall girl, "and this is Jeanette."

Jeanette accepted her handshake, but Estella started firing questions. "Why are you starting to entertain men in January? It's barely August."

"Madame Eugenia doesn't think she will be able to handle it," Linda was quick to respond, before she looked at the two girls. "She's a virgin. Madame Eugenia probably doesn't want her to faint when she sees her first cock. Dearest Ruby wouldn't be good for business then."

The three girls giggled, making Ruby feel like a fool.

"I can speak for myself." Ruby's voice was cold. "Waiting until January, is just a stepping stone. Once I'm upstairs, I'll make the most money out of all of you, you'll see."

Estella placed her hands on her narrow hips. "And what are you planning on doing with all that money, Miss High and Mighty?"

"Open my own brothel," Ruby said proudly, glad her voice wasn't shaking. She had a feeling these girls would tear her apart the minute they saw weakness. "Be just like Madame Eugenia." *Except richer and with much better taste. Something luxurious, but tasteful.*

The girls seemed impressed by her goals. Jeanette pressed a finger on her bottom lip. She kind of reminded Ruby of a cherub. "Be an independent woman? You don't want a husband and children? Madame Eugenia is married, after all."

"But she handles everything; she's smart. Frank is just the heavy hand," Linda pointed out.

"Being dependent on men, has brought me nothing but hardship." Ruby looked at her feet, thinking of her drunk father and how she had acted more like a mother, cleaning up after him, than a daughter. "I have no interest in husbands or babies. Besides, husbands are cruel and babies cry a lot."

Estella nodded in agreement as she shoved Jeanette with her elbow. "See, Ruby is smart. You should be more like her." She rolled her eyes as Jeanette turned red. "This fool still believes her white knight will come for her after he pays to bury himself in her ass."

"It could happen," Jeanette protested weakly, looking at Ruby for support. Ruby happened to agree with Estella, but Jeanette looked so pathetic, and she hated Estella.

"You never know." Ruby placed her hand on her hips. "Stranger things have happened. Madame Eugenia said one of you has to let me borrow clothes until I make enough money to buy my own."

"I'm too short." Jeanette looked apologetic. "But you could have one of my nightgowns."

"Your bottom is too heavy and the size of your chest will rip the buttons." Estella sniffed.

Linda gave a long-suffering sigh. "I guess you'll borrow clothes from me, but I'd better not see a single stain or rip. Come along, Ruby."

"Do you know every chit here?" Dr. Hugh Bennington, his younger brother, smirked when a tall girl gave Steve a flirty look from one of the card tables. Hugh slapped the bottom of a short, plump prostitute wearing a green dress, making her squeal at the impact. Hugh grinned. He and his twin sister Poppy were known in their family as the "Evil Twins" because both of them enjoyed getting under people's skin in a bad way. It was probably why Poppy was still unmarried despite being in her mid-twenties.

"Something like that." Steve's eyes scanned the brothel. It was barely eight, but it was already packed with hardworking men, losing their money on cards, drinks, or between the sheets.

More working girls threw Steve flirty looks or squeezed his upper arms. When his father had died earlier that year, Steve's method of grieving was burying himself between the thighs of every girl in Madame Eugenia's brothel, sometimes two at a time. As a result, everyone in the brothel was beyond friendly to the sheriff.

Steve hardly noticed them; he was only interested in a blonde who had hair like Goldilocks and who had a sharp tongue. His eyes glared at the staircase. Was she already upstairs faking her screams as a dirty miner or low-level farmer pounded into her? The brothel had barely opened its doors, so how the hell had she gotten a client already?

"This would be easier if you would tell me exactly whom we are looking for. You have a crazy look in your eye. It reminds me of Christopher," Hugh argued in a bored tone as he handed a coin to one of the barmaids and accepted a glass of beer.

The piano was starting to play louder, which irritated Steve. He was close to shutting the entire place down if it meant he could search for Ruby in peace, without worrying she was being forced to do something for money.

"Steve?" Hugh raised an eyebrow in annoyance. "Name?"

"Ruby. Ruby Green." His lips thinned. "She barely reaches above my stomach. She has blonde hair, green eyes, and freckles."

"Do you know her?" Hugh laughed. "Why are you so worked up about a little chit?"

"I'm not worked up."

"You're doing a bad job of showing it. Has the great Steve Bennington finally met his match? Is this the girl who is going to tame your womanizing ways?"

Steve didn't agree, but he didn't deny it, either.

All he knew, was that Ruby had driven him crazy since the second he'd laid eyes on her. The minute she opened those pretty pink lips, he knew he would be bewitched by anything she said.

Steve was starting to regret bringing Hugh in the first place. He was a pain in the ass the majority of the time, not to mention he and Poppy seemed to struggle with the concept of feelings. But there had been no one else, and he needed someone to prevent him from acting like a bull in a China shop.

He couldn't bring his sisters to a brothel, his older brother Christopher was happily married and preferred to spend time with his mail order bride, and his other younger brother Anthony was on summer break before he returned for his last year of divinity school. God and whores did not mix. So, it only left Hugh, with his dry humor.

"I need two beers, a glass of whisky, and two bourbons."

Steve moved his head so fast, he was surprised he didn't break his neck. Hugh noticed because he choked on a laugh as he patted Steve's shoulder. "Have fun with Goldilocks. Call me when she kicks you in the balls."

Steve ignored him as he approached the bar where two women were filling drinks while Ruby waited to serve them. Thank goodness she was working downstairs. Barmaids never went upstairs, which meant, for tonight, at least, she wasn't pleasing men. He could feel his blood pressure dropping.

Hugh muttered something underneath his breath about looking for a warm body to lie under. Steve wanted to smack him. He didn't want Ruby to think he thought the same way even though, let's face it, he had run through all the whores in Madame Eugenia's fine establishment at least once.

Ruby was dressed in a dark green dress, which was slightly too short for her if she leaned forward in a certain direction Steve could see her slim ankles and dirty shoes with the little heels which had seen better days.

The blonde had pulled down the front of the dress slightly, giving the patrons a glimpse of the bloody red corset she had underneath which held her heaving breasts. Steve wanted to cover her up then bury his face in those pillowy soft breasts in private.

Ruby was too busy arguing with one of the workers behind the counter, she hadn't noticed when Steve walked by and landed a hard slap on her skirt-covered bottom. A yelp escaped her lips which Steve thought was rather adorable.

The girl rubbed the sore spot on her nates while glaring at him. If looks could kill, Steve would already be dead. "Sheriff," she greeted flatly. "Fancy seeing you here. Didn't anyone tell you it's bad manners to touch a lady you have no relation to?"

"I'm afraid when working at a whorehouse, you can expect all of a man's manners to go out the window." Steve's grin was huge. It was hard to be in a sour mood when he had received confirmation she wasn't underneath a dirty man who was grunting and sweating above her. "What are you doing here? When I met you, you were bragging about being the best painted lady money could buy. I must say, I'm disappointed seeing you here serving drinks like a common waitress."

Ruby flushed bright pink, obviously annoyed by his teasing. Christ, this little lass could be more uptight than his younger sister, Poppy. Maybe his pole up her butt would help her relax a little. He had a feeling she could be quite sweet when she wanted to be.

"It's only for a few months," she huffed. "Only until my birthday, on January first. Madame Eugenia wants to make sure I don't run off like a fool. Like bedding a man would scare me."

January first was still a few months away. It was barely August, after all, so that gave Steve until Christmas at least to think about what he was planning on doing with little Ruby Green. He didn't consider himself a romantic, but he was positive there would be some kidnapping involved.

He wasn't sure if Ruby was a virgin or not. Sometimes, she gave the impression of someone who had bedded a dozen men, then other times, she seemed to be a fumbling mess, not knowing what she was doing half the time.

But Steve was persistent. If anything else, he would strip Ruby of all her secrets one by one even if it killed him.

"Don't you fret. New Years' Day will be here before you know it." Steve's voice was edged with sarcasm as he pulled out a coin and placed it between her pale, plump breasts. "Here, consider this an advance. Save me a spot in the line of men you are expecting to wait for you. By that time, there will probably be half a dozen prettier whores to take your place."

Ruby scowled at him, but her eyes went towards the coin between her breasts. "What is this? I don't need your pity!"

Steve laughed, but there was no humor in it. It was hollow. "It's not pity, sweetheart. Think of it as a down payment. Who knows? Maybe you'll keep it to think of me."

"A down payment?" she asked grouchily.

"Yes." He tipped her chin forward to make her stare at him. "By accepting this coin, you swear I will be the first man who makes love to you on January first."

"My, my, aren't we feeling possessive over a complete stranger?"

"Very," he growled. He was tempted to kiss her, but she would probably slap him. "Do I have your word?"

Ruby bit her bottom lip as she stared at the coin. She obviously wanted to keep it. "It depends, what if I don't do as you say?"

Steve laughed. He had never met such an unruly female with zero preservation skills. "Then, my dear, you will find yourself over my knee, getting your sweet bottom roasted."

Chapter 3

"Did you call for me, Madame Eugenia?" Ruby stepped into the madame's overly perfumed office.

"Yes, I did, child." Madame Eugenia blew her nose with a handkerchief. It seemed everyone at the brothel had been getting sick over the winter holidays. "Close the door; we have something to discuss."

Ruby did as she was told. She had learned quickly that the easiest way to Madame Eugenia's heart was to be obedient and bite her tongue. Both things, she struggled with. She had never had to answer to anyone but herself, and her father had been more drunk than sober, so she had never had to deal with anyone trying to discipline her.

"Yesterday was your birthday," Madame Eugenia commented softly, pressing a hand to Ruby's flushed cheeks. "Nineteen. A beautiful age to be. I am a woman who honors her word, so I ask you again, dear Ruby, is working upstairs something you truly want?"

"Yes!" Ruby answered quickly.

She was tired of working as a barmaid and being

pinched on the bottom for not delivering drinks fast enough, or worse, being hounded by the sheriff who, every third day, pestered her by asking if she didn't want to work anywhere else. She would have thought he would be bored by now, but he was persistent.

One evening, Ruby had snapped at him and demanded to know if he did this with every woman who entered the brothel. The question had quickly shut him up and he had looked displeased, but he hadn't asked her to leave once since the incident. Ruby counted it as a triumph.

Besides, this wasn't about Steve; this was about finally moving upstairs and making money, like Jeanette, Linda, and Estella. She was tired of feeling like a poor church mouse with her meager earnings.

Madame Eugenia nodded, not surprised by her answer. "How would you feel about hosting an auction, dear?"

"An auction?"

"You are a virgin in a brothel; it might as well be the second coming of Christ." The madame's lips twitched. "We could receive quite a hearty sum, you and I, if we auction off your virginity."

Ruby hesitated, not because she would have to sleep with a wealthy man, it was part of her job description after all, but because she had promised her first night to someone else. The sheriff. When he had slipped the coin in between her breasts, he had made her promise she would save herself for him or risk a spanked bottom.

She had never been spanked and she wasn't about to start now. Besides, she had a feeling he hadn't been fibbing when he had made the promise.

"Is something wrong, Ruby?"

"Um, yes I sort of promised the sheriff he could be my first customer," she confessed under her breath.

Madame Eugenia rubbed her chin. "Well, it wouldn't be

such a bad thing if you warmed the sheriff's bed. He has plenty of money. He is a Bennington, after all, you could do worse." A mischievous look crossed her face. "Or you could make him fight for it. Nothing drives men wild more than a little battle among men. Make him work for your sweet little quim, Ruby, or he will get bored."

Ruby hesitated. "Are you saying do the auction and have him bid more than he promised me?"

"Of course." Madame Eugenia's laugh was loud. "You aren't betrothed, girl. This is a whorehouse, even he'll understand. Besides, don't you want to make money?"

The blonde nodded. Perhaps the madame was right and she was being foolish waiting for Steve. Her reputation had been ruined since birth, when she had been born to a whore mother and no-good, drunk daddy. It wasn't like Steve Bennington, who came from a successful ranch family, was going to marry her.

Anyway, it would do the sheriff good to know no one owned Ruby Green and she could do as she pleased.

"All right, we'll do the auction tonight."

"Excellent." Madame Eugenia's eyes were twinkling. "You won't be sorry, honey. After tonight, you and I will be very rich women."

"I have to go." Steve tossed a few coins down, paying for his and his older brother Christopher's drinks. He finished his whisky in one quick swipe and then winked at the busty saloon girl who giggled.

Out of all the Bennington men, Steve had always had the most success with women, often being called somewhat of a Casanova who refused to marry. He was flirty, charming, and, best of all, always knew what to say. Flirting with women, came easy for him, unlike his brothers. Christopher was too uptight, Hugh had the charm of a dead fish, and Anthony was too shy. But Steve always managed to have women wrapped around his little finger.

All except one.

Ruby.

The little blonde had been in Larkspur Valley for five months and she was still as cold as ever. Even with him flirting with her nearly every night, she hadn't cracked and still regarded him as a pest.

It was a little insulting.

"Now? It's barely eight." Christopher frowned. The saloon was barely getting full. This was the first time the brothers had spent time together in the past few months. In August, Christopher's sweet mail order bride, Lucy, had gotten into a bit of a trouble with a person of her past, and as a result, Christopher had been keeping her on a tight leash.

"I have to go. Besides, we both know you were planning on leaving soon to be with your wife."

Christopher and his sister-in-law were almost disgustingly in love, but he was glad his older brother had someone he could be open with. And he had no interest in telling him about Ruby. As far as Chris knew, this was just another example of his womanizing ways.

The only other one who knew about Ruby was Hugh, but Steve had threatened him to keep his mouth shut. Otherwise, he would tell Christopher about how the doctor was bedding every widow in town.

Christopher still didn't look pleased with him; in fact, he was starting to look suspicious. "You've been awfully busy lately in the evenings. Any reason why?"

Ignoring the question, he pointed to Finn Weston, a friend from their youth and Chris's right hand man at the ranch. He was currently nursing a drink and looking miserable, no doubt thinking about their younger sister, Poppy, and the many times she had rejected him. "Why don't you spend some time with Finn? Finn! Come join my brother for a drink."

Once he had safely left his brother in the capable hands of Finn, he made his way to the brothel, which was looking unusually festive. He wondered what was going on. There wasn't a holiday close as far as he knew. But the brothel was decorated with several lanterns and paper streamers, giving the place a cheery atmosphere despite the purpose of it.

A large crowd of men had gathered outside, more than Steve was used to seeing. They were already loud and causing a large ruckus, some of them already completely drunk.

He frowned, wondering if he would have to get involved. He came here to enjoy his peace, not to continue working. He wondered if Madame Eugenia had some sort of promotion going on. She was an excellent businesswoman and her girls were making her richer every day.

"What's going on?" he asked a lanky boy who couldn't be older than eighteen.

The boy blushed as he nervously tugged on his ear. "Nothing much, Sheriff, Madame Eugenia is hosting an auction."

"Oh?" Steve raised an eyebrow in curiosity. Madame Eugenia rarely did auctions. The men around here just didn't have that kind of money to spend on women. "Which girls is she auctioning off?"

"Just one girl, Miss Ruby." The boy had the audacity to blush. "Madame Eugenia is offering the honor of taking her virginity to the highest bidder. Can you believe a girl as beautiful as Ruby being a maiden, Sheriff? Why, if I had more than twenty-five cents in my pocket, I would ask her to marry me and get her away—"

Steve ignored the boy's lovesick woes as anger erupted in his veins. Ruby had promised her maidenhood to him! He would have made sure she had a loving first time, which was what every woman deserved. It was the main reason why he had visited the brothel every day, to make sure the lecherous men kept their hands to themselves.

And now, she was offering her virginity to the highest bidder! Ruby might act tough and might live in a brothel, but she obviously had no idea how sex worked. It would be like sending a lamb to the slaughter if he allowed any of these men to take her innocence away.

Steve forced his way inside, where he saw Ruby perched on the stage where the piano usually was. Her long, blonde hair was loose over her shoulders and she was wearing a see-through white dress which was practically a nightgown, with a bloody red corset over it, cinching her waist tightly.

Despite the heavy powder and rouge she wore on her face, he could tell she was terrified. Her green eyes moved around nervously as men shouted numbers at her as if they were fighting over a prize pig at the market.

Madame Eugenia was standing on the side, obviously enjoying herself as she smoked a pipe. She let out a hearty laugh as if Ruby wasn't about to faint. "At ease, gentlemen, one at a time. Now, where did we leave off? Ah, yes, Mr. Humphry offered twenty-five dollars. Do I hear thirty?"

"Thirty-two dollars!" A toothless man who could be her grandfather offered.

"Thirty-four dollars!"

"Thirty-five dollars!"

"Five hundred dollars!" Steve roared as he glared at the other men, letting them know he would gladly pummel them if they interfered. No one did. Very few people in Larkspur

Valley had that kind of money lying around, and if they did, they would not spend it on a common whore.

Thankfully, Steve came from a wealthy ranching family and his father had left him some money after he passed last year, which his older brother had taught him to use to invest in properties both in Larkspur Valley and in neighboring towns.

Madame Eugenia gaped in surprise and even Ruby looked stunned before a guilty look crossed her face. The little brat probably knew she was going to get an earful. The kind which ended with her over his lap.

"Five hundred, going once, five hundred, going twice, sold to Sheriff Steve Bennington. Sheriff, come here and collect your prize!"

The men parted ways and let Steve in, looking at him with a mixture of respect and annoyance that he had snatched Ruby. If any one of them asked him how she was in bed, he would gladly tell their sweethearts the kind of questions they were asking him.

Steve made his way upstage and picked her up as if she were a new bride. Ruby squeaked but didn't say anything as she wrapped her arms around his neck.

"You're in trouble, little girl," he hissed in her ear, "where's your room?"

"Upstairs," she whispered. "Third door on the left."

Steve nodded as he took her upstairs, ignoring the hollering and whistles behind him. He wanted to shut the entire place down.

Neither of them made a sound as Steve made his way into Ruby's yellow room, which was no bigger than a broom closet. He barely fit, with his large body. He placed Ruby on the bed and then threw her a reproachful look. "You promised."

"I did no such thing." She pushed a blonde wave away

from her face, a haughty look in her eye. "Besides, I do not owe you anything, Sheriff."

"So you made that clear. Perhaps I should throw you to the wolves downstairs."

Silence.

"That's what I thought." He gripped her slim ankle and pushed up her dress, letting him know she was naked underneath. Her mound was covered in delectable, soft, blonde curls. Her tight quim was pink and perfect. He wanted to run his tongue and fingers through the delicate petals of her sex.

Ruby, meanwhile, didn't seem to appreciate that he was admiring her beauty. Instead, she had turned a bright red and started kicking him like an angry horse. "What the hell are you doing, Sheriff?"

"Getting my money's worth. I did pay five hundred dollars for you." He grinned sadistically as he managed to catch her foot with his hand while he used his other one to rip the dress and corset off her, leaving her exposed.

His cock twitched inside his trousers and he feared he would spill himself inside of them before he could properly claim her. Her body was just as pretty as her face. Small and perfect. Her entire body was shaking as she crossed her arms, shielding her bosom, which only made the small breasts pushed up, which fully intrigued him.

Steve gently removed her arms away so he could attend to her pretty little breasts properly. He kissed the left one before he nipped the soft pink nipple between his teeth.

Ruby stopped fighting him as she groaned in both pain and pleasure when she felt his teeth caress her poor nipple. Her hands started roaming through his black hair. As a reward, Steve sucked on her nipple, removing the sting.

Ruby felt her anger melt away as he attended to her breasts. Who knew they would feel so good inside his mouth.

He alternated between gently nipping at them with his teeth and running his hot tongue over them.

A whimper escaped her lips as she arched her hips forward so her mound was rubbing against his lower region. His manhood stirred in his trousers and she could feel it jump against her thigh. It felt weird, but also oddly pleasant.

She had often heard the girls joking about how men were often ruled by their cocks and she didn't doubt it was true. The "thing" seemed to have a mind of its own.

It seemed to be growing especially hard, the more he played with her breasts. Steve's hand lowered to her mound and then to her parted lips. His rough fingers gently parted the puffy flesh as he started stroking her engorged clit.

Up.

Down.

Sideways.

Ruby gasped. She was no stranger to playing with herself, but this was the first time a man had touched her there. She hadn't expected it to be so wonderful.

She felt her nectar seep down her legs and onto his palm and she was in too much bliss to notice or feel embarrassed.

Steve, however, noticed right away. "I think the lady doth protest too much." He brought his fingers to his lips and started sucking on each of them. "Tasty."

Ruby blushed bright red as she stuttered a response, not making a lick of sense.

"You taste exactly like strawberries."

"I eat a lot of strawberries," she replied stupidly. Ruby didn't know if he was trying to charm her or make fun of her.

Steve let out a loud laugh. "See, Ruby, you won't make it as a whore. You might be a hellcat, but you're sweet, not to mention ignorant about what it means to be a soiled dove."

Ruby glared at him, angry at his mocking way. "I thought

you purchased me to sample the goods," she informed him coldly. "If you can't manage it despite your money, Sheriff, then perhaps I should get someone who will take me on a romp in the haystack."

Steve's good humor was erased as he looked at her darkly. "I am trying to be nice."

"I don't want nice. I want you to do what you paid to do."

Steve laughed again, and this time, it was humorless. "You asked for this, Ruby, don't say I didn't warn you."

Ruby couldn't help but widen her eyes when she saw him start to undress. The first thing she caught a glimpse of was a muscled chest covered in curly, black hair, like a large bear. This wasn't the first time she had seen a man's chest, but it was the first time she had seen one which looked so nice.

Down, came his pants and underthings. Before Ruby knew it, she had Steve's erection staring her in the face. Large. Thick. Veiny. A mixture of red and pink. It almost felt like he could eat her alive.

"Not so mouthy now, huh?" he asked wryly.

He gripped the back of her blonde hair and pushed her forward. Ruby opened her mouth to protest, but before she could, he shoved his cock inside her mouth.

Ruby choked as she felt his warm, thick member between her cheeks. It barely fit.

"Suck," Steve ordered lazily, his hand still gripping the back of her head gently.

Ruby glared at him, but willingly did as she was told. She started sucking him off, her pussy throbbing as she ran her tongue down the base of his cock. It was an odd sensation, but not necessarily unpleasant.

Every once in a while, Steve would give her a few pointers while gently massaging her scalp.

"You're going too slow; go fast."

"No teeth, sweetheart, unless you enjoy the taste of blood."

"Excellent. You're doing good. Do that again for me, honey."

Ruby was starting to enjoy the taste of him in her mouth —a mixture of sweetness and saltiness, much like their own personalities.

Then, all of a sudden, he pulled her back.

Ruby looked at him, confused. "Are you done?"

He chuckled. "Not even close, sweetheart, but I want to finish inside you, not inside your pretty little mouth, and I think you've lubed me already."

Ruby nodded, pretending to understand what the hell he was talking about. The girls had given her a few pointers, but she had been so nervous, she hardly remembered them at all.

As if reading her mind, Steve sighed and shook his head slightly as he wrapped his arms around her waist. He lay down on her tiny bed, but pulled her close until she was straddling his chest, her womanhood, which seemed to have become a wet, sloppy mess, rubbing against his chest hair.

"It will hurt less if you are on top of me, Ruby," Steve said seriously. "That way, you can control how fast or how slow we go. But it *is* your first time, meaning it will hurt. We can go fast and get rid of your maidenhood swiftly, or we can—"

"Fast."

"Are you sure?"

"Yes, just get it over with, please."

Steve looked doubtful but didn't argue with her as he gripped her by her hips and pulled her up, before pushing her down on the mushroom head of his cock.

Ruby was being forced to widen, to accept his full length. She let out a cry as she felt a sharp pain in her lower regions, her lips trembling with pain as he pulled out. She saw the blood, her virginal blood, coating his cock and her inner thighs.

Ruby looked at him with big, green eyes, forcing herself not to cry. She must not have been doing a very good job because Steve looked at her with pity as he rubbed her cheek. "Poor baby. I know the first time hurts like hell."

"Did your first time hurt?"

"No." He laughed. "It doesn't hurt for men."

"Figures."

He kissed her bottom lip. "You want me to make you feel good?"

The girl hesitated but, eventually, nodded.

Steve grinned at her as if he had just found her weakness. He quickly placed his hands around her waist again and pushed her down on the bed, so that, this time, her back was lying on the mattress. His strong forearms were against each of her sides, caging her in.

His face was leaning down to her, so close to a kiss, she could almost taste it. As if reading her thoughts, Steve moved forward, placing a dainty kiss on her lips. Even though the touch lasted less than five seconds, she savored every bit of it. The warmness, the softness, the slight hint of soap. Ruby had been kissed before, but it had never been as pleasant as when Steve first kissed her.

Steve looked at her in amusement as he settled between her thighs. "You seem happier about a kiss than about me making you into a woman."

"Well, being kissed doesn't hurt."

Steve didn't disagree with her there. He started landing soft kisses around her neck and clavicle, his lips leaving behind a trail of warmth as his hands disappeared between her legs. A whimper escaped her lips when he found her clit. Just a mere touch, seemed to make her buck her hips like a wild pony.

"Good girl," Steve murmured as he started entering her slowly. "I know it hurts, but I will make you feel good. I promise." He started rubbing her clit with every inch he buried inside her.

She was still incredibly sore, but it felt better now that her hymen was out of the way, and he was being gentle with her.

"My Lord, you're beautiful, Ruby," Steve praised, his eyes filled with lust.

"I know," Ruby panted as his strokes became faster. This time, her hips rocked against his with each motion of his thrust. He was filling her with every inch of his cock. It should have hurt, given how sore she was, but it didn't. She felt so good, she almost saw stars.

Steve looked amused as he circled his thumb against her clit before rubbing it slowly. "You're not humble at all, are you?"

"No, why should I be?"

"Well, you have a point."

Ruby felt her heart beating rapidly as he pummeled into her faster, until their hips were bumping each other. Ruby dug her nails against his back as her first orgasm provided by a man overwhelmed her.

Her entire body shook with her pleasure as she settled on the mattress, a tired, but satisfied look on her face. She felt Steve's warm seed coating her pussy and inner thighs.

She wanted to smack herself for letting him finish inside her. She was running the risk of getting pregnant. The girls had warned her not to let clients finish inside her without her device, but Steve had been too handsome for her to resist. Ruby would never make that mistake again.

He smirked at her as he nibbled on her neck. "How was that? Better?"

Ruby nodded.

Steve looked pleased with the answer as he puffed up his

chest like a proud rooster. Men. They were all the same. He sat down on the edge of the bed, hopefully to dress, because she was feeling tired.

"Good." Before Ruby could snuggle against the soft covers for some much-needed sleep, she found herself being pulled from the bed and placed over his lap, completely naked.

Her brain froze, not registering what had just happened. Why had the sheriff placed her over his lap? Was it something perverted? How was he not tired?

Before she could even open her mouth, his hand landed harshly on her rump, leaving behind a bright red handprint. She squeaked in pain at the sting left behind. Had he actually slapped her ass when she was face down?

She had just finished the thought when a second slap landed on the other cheek. She now had two decorative handprints decorating her ass. Worst of all, both slaps had hurt.

"What the hell are you doing, Bennington?"

Ruby tried to pull away, but he had an impressive grip around her waist as the punishing strokes continued to rain down with gusto, not caring that she was obviously displeased about them.

"Punishing you," he answered her calmly as his hand continued to fall down on her upturned rear. "If you don't want me to wash your pretty little mouth with soap, take your spanking like a good girl."

"Why are you spanking me?" she whined, kicking her legs like an angry pony as he continued blistering her ass.

"Because you broke your promise. You promised you were going to save yourself for me, but instead, you turned around and started auctioning yourself to the highest bidder. Now, your ass is paying the price."

The sound of his loud smacks ran through the small living room, his hand digging into her soft flesh.

"I did no such thing!"

"You took the coin I placed between your breasts on your first day."

"You didn't hear me say yes, now did you, idiot?"

But Steve didn't seem to care about the technicalities, because he was only focused on blistering her bottom by landing his hand down as hard as he could until her skin glowed red. At first, Ruby tried to struggle, but when she saw it was useless, she gave up and, instead, just cried, naked, over his lap. The man had taken her virginity and spanked her all in the same hour.

After what seemed like the thirtieth stroke, Steve stopped spanking her and delivered her to her bed, not caring that Ruby was a crying mess. She rubbed her very sore cheeks angrily, but the heat didn't diminish. It felt like her whole ass was burning.

Ruby let out a low wail as she grabbed a nearby pillow. With one hand still rubbing her ruby-red cheeks, she threw the pillow at Steve's handsome face. "Get out!"

Chapter 4

RUBY SLEEPILY TURNED AROUND, going from lying down on her belly to her sore cheeks pressing against the mattress. A groan escaped her lips as she remembered how she had been embarrassingly spanked over Steve's lap yesterday before he left her there crying without even a kiss goodbye.

A small pouch filled with coins and bills had been delivered on her nightstand, no doubt the work of Madame Eugenia. She had probably left the money in her room after she had cried herself to sleep. But not even the money seemed to make her happy this morning.

Ruby was sore all over. Her bottom hurt and there was an empty ache between her legs. She couldn't hide her winces as she walked to the washroom to take a bath.

Why did her first night have to be with a literal giant? There was still some dry blood on her thighs from when she had refused to let Steve clean her the night before, which only reminded her of the way his thick, heavy member had parted her open inch by inch, until he took her virginity.

The few moments of pleasure had been erased when her hot, spanked bottom had been pressed against the mattress, reminding her that he had spanked her like a disobedient child for not saving her first for him only, instead auctioning herself off. Being spanked, was not something she appreciated in the least.

As she poured cold water into the tub for her morning bath, she couldn't help but stare at herself in the nearby mirror. She had expected to look more womanly, but she still felt like the simple-minded girl she had been only yesterday.

Her skin was pale while her blonde hair stuck to her forehead in odd angles. Finger marks belonging to Steve, from the way he had gripped her hips, adorned her skin. But what most reminded her of last night, were her ruby red cheeks which were still swollen from last night's punishment. The handprints were even painted on them as a mocking gesture.

"Ow," she groaned as her fingers touched the tight skin hoping to soothe it, but it was clear she was not going to be able to sit down properly for at least a week.

Damn him! The next time she saw him, she was going to make him sorry for ever spanking her!

Once she finished her bath, Ruby headed downstairs for breakfast, which she was going to have to eat standing up. The rest of the girls were in various stages of undress as they bit into pieces of toast or cut into their eggs.

Estella tightened her robe as she looked in Ruby's direction. "Look who came downstairs dressed with every button buttoned nice and tight. There's no use in pretending you are still a straight-laced virgin, honey."

Linda winked. "We've heard the screams. Everyone here has had the sheriff at least once. I told you he was the best man to have in your bed the first time."

The women giggled while Ruby turned bright red. It took every ounce of her composure not to slap them both.

Jeanette looked at her nervously as she handed her a cup

of tea. "Here, Ruby, it's chamomile tea. It helps your body when you're feeling sore."

Ruby smiled, silently thanking her. Jeanette was the only one she liked in this terrible establishment, with the exception of Madame Eugenia. "Did you remember to use your device last night?"

Ruby froze. Linda had given her a small contraceptive device simply known as the "womb veil" a few days ago. She had even given her an embarrassing demonstration of how to insert it. Ruby still didn't quite know how it worked. All she knew was it was supposed to prevent a man's seed from getting inside her so she didn't become pregnant.

"I forgot," she confessed.

Linda shook her head as she gulped her coffee. "It would be your sorry luck if you got a bun in the oven from the first time you had sex."

"Just don't forget to use it from now on, Ruby," Jeanette made her promise.

"Maybe it would be a good thing." Estella looked at her over her slim shoulder. "The sheriff is clearly smitten with you. Why would he waste so much money on a common whore? He has never spent such a large amount on us after all." Estella gave her a simpering smile. "Maybe your luck is changing, Ruby, and the sheriff will get you wed before you know it. He already bedded you; you'll probably be popping out kids for him every year."

"Christopher Bennington married a poor girl from Boston last year," another woman named Bella pointed out. "The sheriff marrying Ruby wouldn't be as far-fetched, especially since she hasn't slept with half of the town like the rest of us."

The women broke out into hearty chuckles.

"I am not marrying Steve Bennington," Ruby growled. "Honestly, all of you are acting as if he owns me already."

Linda gave her an eyeroll. "Sweetheart, don't be stupid. All of us saw how he looked at you. No man spends five hundred dollars for a woman he just wants to fool around with under the sheets. Mark my words, this will be your final day here."

Ruby got up from the breakfast table angrily while the women looked at her with amusement. With the exception of Jeanette, they had all been treating her horribly since her first day. Some thought her attitude was too high and mighty to belong to a whore, but the majority of them were jealous of her beauty.

She made her way to Madame Eugenia's office, where she and Frank were arguing over bills. They stopped when they looked at Ruby. "Yes? I thought you were still lying in bed."

"No." Ruby cleared her throat. "I was wondering if I could still entertain this evening?"

Frank and Madame Eugenia exchanged looks. "I thought you would be too sore."

"No. Why?"

Madame Eugenia's lips curled into a smirk. "Frank and I thought the sheriff was rather sweet on you."

"I heard wedding bells," Frank continued sarcastically.

"Well, he's not," Ruby snapped. "He's slept with half of the whores here. Why am I so different? Can I entertain or not?"

Madame Eugenia pulled out a long box and picked up one of the thick cigars. "You are not just beautiful and cold. Ruby, you're also highly oblivious, but yes, you may serve."

Later in the evening, Ruby descended down the stairs wearing a daring red dress with a black corset which was cinched so tightly, she could hardly breath. Not to mention, her breasts felt crushed against the thick material.

She tried to keep the smile on her painted lips, but a hiss

parted from her lips every time her drawers rubbed against her punished flesh. The redness had diminished somewhat, but it still felt achy.

The brothel was already lively with music and drink. Her eyes darted across the room in search of the sheriff, but she could not find him. Perhaps she had been right and he had gotten bored after all.

The blonde tried to ignore the stabbing pain in her chest at the thought. She didn't know why she cared so much. Perhaps it was because he had been the man who had taken her virginity. No wonder she was so sentimental.

A large hand grabbed her fleshy hip and spun her around. A middle-aged man was grinning at her. He was missing a tooth, had a bushy beard, and his plaid shirt, though clean, was wrinkled. Ruby was disappointed. He could be her father!

Still, she forced a smile on her face and fluttered her eyelashes. "How do you do? I'm Ruby."

"Mighty good, Miss Ruby. I'm Todd. My day might be better with some companionship for the evening. Especially with a pretty lady."

Ruby gave him a high price, hoping he would refuse. He didn't. Instead, he promptly gave the money to Madame Eugenia and whisked her away upstairs. Ruby kept looking over her shoulder almost stupidly, hoping Steve would walk through the doors of the brothel and pull her away.

But he didn't.

Ruby closed her eyes. This had been her choice, and now she had to stick to it. She hadn't wanted to be like her mama —saddled to a no-good man, which left her with no choice but to sell her body, and it had resulted in her death. Men caused trouble. They were only after a woman's body.

Steve was no different. He might whisper pretty things in her ear, but at the end of the day, he was still just a man.

Sex with Todd was different than sex with Steve. Even when Steve was angry with her, he was still passionate and gentle despite his roughness in brief periods. He cared about her pleasure and made her cry out with need even as he squeezed her spanked cheeks.

Todd was just rough in general. He pumped into her even though she had still been dry. His hands were squeezing her breasts so roughly, she was surprised he didn't leave bruises behind. Fifteen minutes later, Todd went downstairs whistling happily while Ruby made her way behind him, wishing she could have a bath.

She froze on the staircase when she saw Steve at the bottom. He seemed to have been arguing with Frank about something before he stopped to look at Todd's satisfied face and then at Ruby. The sheriff was holding a bouquet of yellow pansies tied with a fat white bow in his hand. It was quite obvious what had happened.

Would he yell? Cause a scene? Spank her?

She felt the guilt settle in her throat and she was afraid she was going to cry. Ruby wanted to tell Steve she hated sleeping with men for money. That it wasn't as easy as she thought it was going to be. But she didn't. Instead, she just kept her mouth shut and forced herself to keep staring at him.

A look of hurt passed through his eyes as he dropped the flowers at the bottom of the staircase, leaving Ruby behind.

The next few days weren't much better for Ruby. When she wasn't entertaining clients upstairs, each one more terrible than the last, she was avoiding the sheriff. He still wasn't speaking to her and she seemed to have lost all her bravado to actually go talk to him.

But like clockwork, he came every night and stayed until the brothel was almost closed. Sometimes he would be so drunk, he got into arguments with other customers. Twice,

Frank had had to kick him out, and three times, his younger brother Hugh had to come for him. The younger brother always threatened with telling their older brother, Christopher, but he never did.

It hurt to watch him.

Hurt to be near him and not touch him or have him tease her like he used to.

She supposed she could have made the first move, but she was too proud to do so. Ruby had slept with twelve men since the night Steve took her virginity, each one worse than the last. One of them had even left a bruise on the back of her neck from how hard he had fucked her against the bedpost.

Ruby was starting to forget how Steve felt when he was on top of her, his warm embraces, soft touch, and his strong muscles shielding her body. By the looks of it, he was never going to sleep with her again.

One week, after she had basically given Steve the middle finger, Ruby found herself at the mercantile looking for cloth to make a new dress. Her clients kept ripping her old ones, and after the week she'd had, she deserved something pretty.

She liked going at noon because it was when most of the town was eating lunch and she could avoid the harsh looks of judgmental women and the lustful looks of men.

Mrs. Simon, whose husband owned the mercantile, refused to serve her because of where she worked. Mr. Simon wasn't much better, always shooing her away as if she had rats crawling in her hair, but at least he didn't give her dirty looks like his wife. In fact, he would always stare at her bosom a little too long.

Men were all the same.

Ruby wondered why women even married at all. She had a feeling they would be happier without any men around. She studied her fingernails as she waited for Mr. Simon to come back from wrapping the cloth in a neat package so she could take it home.

Ruby stiffened when she felt familiar strong hands grip her tiny waist, along with the smell of pine trees and soap. She reluctantly turned around and found herself staring into the eyes of Steve Bennington.

The problem was he didn't look as handsome this morning. In fact, he looked rather worse for wear, as if he hadn't slept in days. Even though his clothes were clean, his eyes were a bloody red and facial hair covered his cheeks and chin. Ruby didn't know if he was drunk or sleep-deprived.

"Ruby," he whispered in her ear, "fancy seeing you here, and without all your suitors waiting around like lovesick puppies. It's practically a miracle."

Steve's comment referred to the men who often followed Ruby whenever she ventured outside of the brothel to do her errands. Some of them were past clients and others were hoping to be future clients, but they couldn't scrimp the money together so they often had to be satisfied with worshipping her from afar.

But as Madame Eugenia often said with glee, 'A whore like Ruby Green is never cheap.' In just a matter of days, she had become one of Madame Eugenia's most expensive girls, much to Estella and Linda's jealousies.

Ruby knew she should be happy. After all, this was what she had wanted, wasn't it? She was making money left and right and all she had to do was let a man poke her and brag about how wonderful he was in bed.

Strangely, though, Ruby felt even more miserable than when she first came here. Not even the money seemed to be enough anymore. She was tired of being manhandled, tired of being told the same compliments about her beauty, and simply exhausted of having men's hands on her. Men who were often much older than she was, didn't shower, or were ugly, with nasty attitudes. Sometimes, all of the above.

But her pride would never let herself admit she was wrong. Not to mention, what kind of job could she obtain that paid as much as opening her legs?

"What are you doing here, shouldn't you be sulking?" she quipped.

It had been what Steve had been doing all this time, pouting angrily as he watched her take men upstairs. This was the first time he had confronted her face to face.

Steve didn't answer. He just kept staring at her like one of her lovesick-puppy suitors.

"What do you want, Sheriff?" Ruby huffed, wondering what was taking Mr. Simon so long. If she hadn't already paid, she would have taken her butt right out of the store. She had a feeling Steve could kill her in public and the rest of this judgmental town would barely blink in her direction, probably glad there was one less whore polluting their precious town.

"You." Steve lowered his head until his chin was pressing against her shoulder. His hands were still resting against her hips, his lips brushing against her neck. "I only want you, Ruby."

Ruby stiffened as his words. Many men had claimed to want her, but none of them sounded as sincere as Steve. She tried to play it off. "My, Sheriff Bennington, is this a proposal?"

"Yes," he admitted. Before Ruby could demand what the hell he meant by that, he continued. "I will pay you whatever you want, double on Sundays, as long as you're exclusively mine. Promise me I will be the only man in your bed, and I will give you whatever you want from me."

Ruby gulped, looking for any traces that he was making fun of her, but he looked pretty serious. He wanted to be exclusive, it would be as if she were a kept woman who was living in a brothel. "I'm an expensive whore," she warned him.

"I have money."

"I don't work on Sundays." Even the brothel closed on holy days. It was truly ironic.

"Monday through Saturday."

Ruby weighed the benefits. On the plus side, she wouldn't have to sleep with ugly, sweaty men ever again, but then she was running the risk of Steve believing he "owned" her, something she definitely didn't want him to feel. Ruby belonged to no one except herself.

"Ruby?"

Mr. Simon chose that moment to come out with her package. He looked confused, probably wondering how one of the town's most infamous whores was speaking to the sheriff. As if Steve were some kind of saint before she had arrived.

"Yes," Ruby murmured so Mr. Simon couldn't hear as she took her package. "I'll be yours."

Chapter 5

TWO MONTHS LATER, Steve found himself lying on Ruby's naked breast as the blonde ran her fingers through his dark hair while he finished making love to her for the third time that evening. Ruby had kept her side of the bargain, and as long as he kept providing her with money, she would willingly spend the night with him.

Of course, it helped that Steve tired her out every night, to the point she had no desire to sleep with any other man. The blonde had rendered him obsessed. He had often teased his big brother Christopher about practically kissing his wife Lucy's feet, and here he was, practically doing the same.

He often found himself thinking about Ruby at all hours, about her shiny blonde hair, her pillowy lips, and her green, cat-like eyes which often shone with mischief. Though she had settled a bit ever since Steve had started spending time with her in the evenings, like a spoiled house cat.

They even managed to have decent conversations in the early hours of the morning instead of arguing all the time. Ruby had gotten into the habit of smoking with him whenever he would share some of his cigar with her.

The early rays of sunlight were poking through her small windows while his shoulders slumped with exhaustion, reminding him he had to go to work in two hours. He was such a welcome sight nearly every night that Madame Eugenia even offered him breakfast every morning before he left for work.

For the past two months, with the exception of Sundays, he would spend the entire night fucking Ruby then head on to work for the rest of the day. The endless cycle had finally taken a toll on him, but Madame Eugenia had been right. Ruby was an expensive whore and he couldn't risk her running off to someone else for a quick buck.

"My sisters are throwing Lucy a surprise birthday party next month."

She raised an eyebrow. "I thought they hated her."

"She softened them up. She's a sweetheart. Lucy is good for my brother."

Ruby nodded. "I'm assuming your whole family is going?"

"Yes." Anthony, the youngest of the brothers, had finished divinity school early and had returned to the small town, to take over the church. "We're finally together again. Anthony and Hugh were away at school for a while, so it will be nice to have them back."

Ruby started rubbing his back with her small hand. "It must be nice to have siblings. I never had anyone."

"They could be your siblings too." He looked at her. "If you ever agree to leave this place and marry me."

Her gaze hardened. "Don't start. I don't want to get into another argument. Anyway, shouldn't you be going? You're going to be late for work."

Steve untangled his body from her arms as he started dressing himself. "I'll see you tonight," he addressed her coldly. This had been the ninth time she had rejected him and he had to admit it still hurt.

Ruby yawned, curling herself against the blankets.

She looked like an adorable doll, too bad she had a heart of stone. A beautiful ice princess.

Steve fought the urge to kiss her. How could she still be so cold after they'd spent weeks in each other's arms? Maybe Hugh was right and she was only an endless money pit to him.

After getting his daily toast and butter from the brothel's cook, he made his way back to the sheriff's office. Much to his surprise, he found his younger brothers, Hugh and Anthony, waiting for him.

Hugh looked bored and was already smoking even though it was barely seven in the morning. Anthony looked nervous and was fidgeting back and forth.

"There he is." Hugh let out a cloud of smoke. "Fresh as a daisy. How much money did she take out of you tonight?"

Steve ignored him as he turned to Anthony, who wasn't a headache like Hugh. "What are you two doing here?"

"We're worried about you, Steve." Anthony bit his lower lip. "You spend every night with Miss Ruby—"

"The whore," Hugh piped in, and Steve wanted to smack him.

"You're exhausting yourself, being with her all night and working all day. Not to mention, you're spending a ridiculous amount of money. You even sold the property Father left you to keep paying for her company." Anthony sounded completely sympathetic.

Hugh raised an eyebrow. "Do you know how Christopher will react when he finds out about all the money you've spent on a little tramp? He will go crazy."

Steve knew for a fact there was a very good chance Christopher would kill him when he found out he was this close to being in debt after being very good with his money, but he still refused to let go of Ruby. To him, Ruby was more precious than money.

Though he doubted his responsible, no-nonsense older brother would understand. He and his wife were crazy for each other. Christopher had never had to beg Lucy for her attention.

"Don't you dare tell him!" Steve hissed at Hugh, "I'm serious, Hugh, not unless you want to lose your pretty teeth."

Hugh didn't blink. "Then stop spending money like a fool. The little whore will not like you any better if you're poor. This is pathetic, you begging for her attention."

Sensing the tension, Anthony stood between them. "You should come to dinner tonight. The girls miss you, they've been asking about their big brother."

Steve suddenly felt ashamed for being so inconsiderate. He didn't mean to ignore Poppy, Iris, and especially the baby of the family, Lily. "I'll go to dinner tonight."

He would eat a quick dinner with his sisters then head on to see Ruby for the rest of the night.

Anthony looked relieved. "We'll see you then."

Hugh didn't look so easily pleased. "I hope this Ruby is worth it. She's costing you everything, Steve. It's like she bewitched you."

Steve arrived clean and freshly shaved to the Bennington's second home. It used to be Christopher's bachelor pad, but when he had married Lucy, the pair had moved to the main house while his unwed sisters had stayed in the smaller house.

Much to his surprise, his sister, Poppy, Hugh's twin sister, was waiting outside for him instead of fussing over the dinner plates. She wore a fawn-colored dress with thick, black horizontal stripes. Every button was buttoned tightly at her throat and she wore a frown on her pretty face.

Christopher and Steve often worried their little sister would remain a spinster forever at twenty-six, but her sour mood and sharp tongue had driven the majority of men away. Poppy had taken over the motherly role and raising of the younger children when Mrs. Bennington had died giving birth to Lily. As a result, she had not paid the proper attention to courting as a young woman probably should.

He grinned at her. "You're here to welcome me home?"

She snorted. "You don't deserve a welcome after you basically ignored us for weeks."

A guilty look spread on his face as he kissed her cheek. "Sorry, little sister. I had some pressing matters. It won't happen again. Now, why don't you tell me why you're waiting outside for me?"

Poppy hesitated before she raised her chin proudly. "Christopher and Hugh are already aware, but I thought you should know. I have a beau now."

Steve raised an eyebrow. "Finn?"

Finn Weston was Christopher's right-hand man at the ranch and he had been hopelessly in love with Poppy since the minute he saw her. Unfortunately for him, Poppy saw Finn as nothing more than dirt on her shoes, even though he had practically begged her to give him a chance.

Steve would have felt bad for him if he wasn't so pathetic. Finn couldn't take a hint even if Poppy was stabbing his heart.

Poppy scowled. "Not Finn. Richard Glass, he works at the post office. He is a very nice, respectable gentleman. Chris has already met him and he approved. He's coming to Lucy's birthday party next month."

Steve had met Richard Glass a handful of times. He was

a nice man, though a bit on the duller side. He was surprised someone as headstrong and assertive as Poppy was interested in him. "Oh, I thought it would be Finn. He's still sweet on you, you know. I thought you had finally given him a chance."

She stiffened. "Finn is Finn. Nothing more. I have no interest in courting him, and neither you nor Chris can force me to."

"We wouldn't dream of it, Pop." He squeezed her hand. "We just want you to be happy. Does he make you happy?"

Poppy nodded, but she struggled to force a smile. Perhaps she was feeling nervous. "Yes, very much so."

"It's all we want for you, Pop." He offered his arm to her. "Now come on, let's have some dinner."

Chapter 6

"OH, WHAT IS IT?"

Estella practically pounced on Ruby the second she came in with a familiar creamy box, which indicated a new dress from the dressmaker.

Linda studied her fingernails, obvious jealousy seething from her. She hadn't been getting as many clients ever since Ruby started flaunting around her beauty. Even though the entire brothel's clientele knew about Ruby's agreement with the sheriff, they were still hopeful they would have a chance with Ruby Green.

"What do you think? A new dress. She's been buying a new one each week, as if she were an English princess."

Ruby ignored her as she removed the big bow sealing the box. It was her money, so she could do as she pleased. Besides, no one had invited the girls to barge into her new room. Madame Eugenia had been so pleased with all the money she had been bringing in, she had upgraded Ruby to the second largest upstairs bedroom.

"Oh, pipe down, Linda. Ruby works hard, she deserves to have nice things." Jeanette threw Ruby a humble smile.

Out of all the girls, she got along with Jeanette the most. Probably because she was so nice and not jealous or catty, like Estella and Linda.

Ruby pulled out the dress excitedly. It was the prettiest dress she owned and she had given the dressmaker specific instructions. It was made of the lightest lavender color, almost white, with expensive transparent silk around the neck and wrist. There was a thick sash around her waist and the dressmaker had even included a matching bow to wear to church on Sunday.

Well, perhaps not church—she was certainly not welcome there—but around town. Definitely with Steve, since he seemed to like frilly, girlish things. He practically requested them every time he joined her in bed.

"Oh, it's beautiful." Jeanette's eyes sparkled. "Put in on, Ruby, please."

Not one to dismiss an adoring audience, Ruby quickly undressed and put the dress on over her underthings while Linda and Estella watched with greed.

"Button me, please?" Ruby asked Jeanette. She was the only one she trusted not to rip the dress apart by "accident."

Jeanette nodded as she started buttoning the back of the dress. She got halfway through when she stopped. She hesitated as she struggled with the material.

Estella and Linda started snickering.

She flushed, her cheeks turning bright red. "What is it?"

Jeanette hesitated. "The top four buttons won't button. Perhaps the dressmaker made a mistake."

"Mrs. Greg never makes mistakes." Linda's lip curled in amusement.

"Perhaps you've simply gotten fat and you refuse to admit it." Estella laughed. "You have been gorging yourselves with chocolate and sweets. Opening your legs, hardly counts as exercise, and you've been spending all your time on your back."

Ruby turned around angrily. "Oh, you shut up! I haven't gained weight."

"Then how do you explain the buttons?" Estella raised an eyebrow. "Unless the sheriff put a baby in you."

"Ruby is not pregnant." Jeanette squeezed her hand. "You've been using your thing, haven't you?"

"Of course." *Most of the time.* This was not the time to tell them that sometimes Steve found himself between her legs before she could place the device inside herself. She placed a hand on her belly. There couldn't possibly be a baby there, could there? "Mrs. Greg probably got my measurements wrong. She's losing her eyesight, you know. Now leave, you three. I'm tired."

"Why didn't you tell me Steve's brother is the only town doctor?" Ruby hissed in Jeanette's ear once the two girls were invited to sit in the small sitting room while the doctor got the examination room ready.

When she had first seen him, she had noticed both men shared similar features, but she had chalked it up to a coincidence. Of course, when the blue-eyed man introduced himself as Dr. Hugh Bennington, all coincidences flew out the window.

Yes, Steve had mentioned his brother was a doctor, but both he and Jeanette had failed to admit he was the only town doctor.

Jeanette bit her lower lip, and Ruby suddenly felt guilty for yelling at her. She had been the one to accompany Ruby after all. "I forgot."

Ruby murmured something under her breath.

"Miss Green, I'm ready for you," Dr. Bennington announced. He had the warmth of an icicle. "Would your friend like to accompany you?"

Ruby nodded.

For the next twenty-five minutes, Ruby underwent a series of embarrassing examinations and questions until Dr. Bennington, in his cold way, finally looked at her with what was supposed to be a smile. "Congratulations, Miss Green, you're with child. From what you discussed with me, I can assume you are about two months pregnant—"

"That's impossible," Ruby hissed.

He blinked. "I could run more tests if you wish, but based on what you told me—the loss of bleeding for two months, the weight gain, and the obvious moodiness—I can assure you, you are carrying a baby in your womb. You could wait a month or so to be truly confirmed, but I doubt it is necessary."

Ruby felt like she was going to faint. In fact, she had to hold on to the chair, to prevent herself from tumbling forward. A baby? She couldn't possibly be pregnant. She had used the device Madame Eugenia had given her. Most of the time. With every one of her clients except Steve.

"Oh, Ruby, didn't you use your device?" Jeanette whispered.

Before she could respond, Hugh spoke for her in his annoying, know-it-all way of his. "No device is truly useful to prevent pregnancy."

Ruby glared at him. Then her hand went to her belly. She could hardly believe there was a baby settled in there. What was she going to do? Who had ever heard of a prostitute with a baby? There was no doubt Madame Eugenia would kick her out of the brothel the second she knew about it.

She imagined telling Steve, but the fool would probably

be overjoyed and drag her to the church before she could even protest.

No, she had to get rid of it. Now. Before she grew any bigger. It was probably the size of a walnut in her belly.

Ruby had no interest in being a wife and mother. Her only goal was to earn her own money independently and eventually open her own brothel and be as successful as Madame Eugenia.

With a clenched jaw, Ruby looked at Hugh, who was barely looking in her direction, already bored. "Do not tell Steve about this. I'm planning on…" she couldn't even say it, "…the baby will not come to fruition."

There, it didn't sound as bad.

Hugh visibly relaxed. It was clear, he wasn't interested in having Ruby for a sister-in-law, either. "Good. It's better like this. My brother, having a baby with the town's most expensive whore, it wouldn't be good for him."

Ruby tried to ignore the sting of his words. What about her? Then again, her reputation had gone in the dirt the second she walked into Madame Eugenia's. She tilted her chin proudly. "How much do I owe you?"

He gave her a wry smile. "Nothing, kid. Save it. You're going to need every penny."

"Maybe you should just keep the baby." Linda popped a strawberry in her mouth as she surrounded Ruby along with Jeanette and Estella. Jeanette had squealed like a piglet about her misfortune the second they returned home, and honestly, Ruby was too stressed to even be bothered.

"Are you out of your mind?" Estella cocked her head as she studied the blonde as if expecting to see a large belly under her gray dress. "Do you honestly think Madame Eugenia will let her stay here? This is no place for a baby."

"I know that, stupid girl." Linda scowled. "I meant, she could get the sheriff to marry her. He is already obsessed with her."

Estella looked doubtful. "There is a difference between bedding a whore and marrying her. Do you think Christopher Bennington will approve of his brother marrying a soiled dove?"

"Well, Christopher Bennington isn't his daddy. The sheriff is a grown man." Linda crossed her arms over her chest. "I think you should think it through. Steve Bennington is an honorable man, unlike some of these fools. He will give you a roof over your head and food in your belly."

Ruby stood up, gripping her gray skirts. She was suddenly tired of all of them. Ruby ignored the girls calling for her as she made her way to Madame Eugenia. She found the madame hunched over papers. If anyone could help her, it would be her boss. She doubted she was the first girl who had gotten herself in this predicament. "What is it, Ruby? I'm busy."

"I need your help."

"To do what?"

Ruby gulped as she crossed her arms over her belly. "To get rid of a baby."

Chapter 7

"WHAT'S WRONG?"

Ruby stiffened as Steve ran a finger down her bare spine. Even though she was nude, they hadn't had sex. She had told him she wasn't feeling well and Steve decided to give her some space.

Currently, Ruby was curled up on the far end of the bed, staring at the wall. Her dress and underthings were on the floor and she had her blanket wrapped around her body tightly. She had hardly looked at Steve since he stepped inside the room and he wondered if he had done something to make her upset.

But they had been laughing and joking yesterday, so he wasn't quite sure what, exactly, she was upset about.

"Nothing."

Steve sighed. "I know you're upset, Ruby. If I did something—"

"Not everything is about you," she accused him coldly, wrapping the blanket tighter around herself.

Steve took a deep breath, begging the Lord to give him

strength. Why did women have to be so complicated? It was like pulling teeth when they were upset. Not pleasant at all.

He leaned forward and kissed the back of her bare shoulder. "I wish you were honest with me."

Ruby pouted. "What's the point?"

"The point is we could solve whatever is troubling you." Steve pulled her into his arms, taking in the strawberry aroma from her skin. Ruby had confessed she often took baths with dry rose petals and cut strawberries, to give her skin their lovely scent. Steve thought it was a waste of perfectly good fruit, but he wasn't opposed to it if it made her happy.

Ruby didn't answer.

"Ruby," he growled in her ear. "What's making you upset? Don't make me ask again. Do you want another spanking?" He clutched one bare butt cheek in his hand, making his point.

Steve hadn't spanked her for months, even though Ruby often deserved a stinging red butt because of her sharp tongue. He was a patient man, but his patience was running thin.

The blonde responded by bursting into tears, startling him and making him feel guilty about how he had demanded an answer of her. He didn't think he had ever seen Ruby cry except when he was spanking her or when he gave her an intense orgasm.

Fat tears rolled down her cheeks as her entire body shook, her bare breasts rubbing against his muscled chest. Steve was so startled, he just held her close, rubbing her bottom with his large hands.

"There, there, honey, it's all right." Steve brushed his lips against her forehead and then her lips. "What is it? What's bothering you? Do you need someone arrested?" he joked.

She shook her head, staring at him with those big green

eyes, which only made Steve want to destroy anyone who would harm her. "I just feel sick."

Steve didn't think she was being overly truthful, but at the same time, he didn't want to push her. "Do you want me to send for tea?" He tightened his arms around her protectively. "Or I could call Hugh to take a look at you."

Panic entered her eyes as she started shaking her head. Perhaps she was afraid of doctors?

"I'm fine. I'm just tired."

Steve lay down on her small bed, pressing her head against his chest as he started stroking her arms. "Sleep, darling, you need it."

The next morning, Steve took his younger sister, sixteen-year-old Iris, to the mercantile to buy supplies for a school project she was working on. While Iris picked up pieces of fabric and placed them in her small wooden basket, Steve looked around, trying to hide his boredom.

Boredom was suddenly the last thing on his mind when a familiar blonde entered the room wearing a gray and rose dress. It looked more raggedy than the new, tight, fashionable dresses she always wore, but then women were always weird when it came to clothes.

Ruby gave him a grimace before shielding her face with her bonnet. They had an unspoken agreement that when they were in public, they did not address each other, but still, she didn't have to look at him like he was dirt on his shoes.

Before Steve could go to tease her, Ruby turned on her heels and basically ran out of the mercantile, a handkerchief across her mouth. The woman grew ever odder, the more he spent time with her. Perhaps she was sick in the head.

"Steve, I'm ready. Are you getting anything for yourself?"

"No." He quickly paid before he helped Iris with her bags. He was going to drop her home, then he was going to return to the office to do some paperwork. Steve interrupted

Iris babbling about her school project to ask her the following, "Iris, what do you think is a nice present for a lady friend?"

If Christopher found out Steve was asking their baby sister about a present for his mistress, he would happily strangle him.

Iris looked surprised. "I didn't know you were courting anyone. Is it someone from church?"

No, but she will possibly make Anthony faint, he thought. "No, but my lady friend has been upset. I want to give her a little gift to make her happy."

Iris looked amused. She probably thought he was a fool. "Candy or flowers are always a nice gesture."

"I want something different. This friend—"

"Steve, can I talk to you?"

Steve and Iris stopped their conversation to look at Christopher's right-hand man, who often felt like an additional brother, Finn. Finn gave Iris a small, apologetic smile before he practically dragged Steve away from her.

"You have a strong grip," Steve hissed once they were away from Iris' curious gaze. "What is it?"

He took a deep breath, as if trying to control his anger. "How could you not tell me Poppy was courting Richard Glass? I had to see them in church together before either you or Chris bothered to tell me."

Steve rolled his eyes. Finn had been obsessed with Poppy ever since he came to work for the Bennington ranch in his late teens. Unfortunately, Poppy did not feel the same way and she had been rejecting him nearly twice a year for as long as he could remember.

He would have found it funny if it wasn't so pathetic. Finn hadn't even tried to move on and, instead, continued to look at Poppy with big cow eyes as he watched her court a few men. Though, this time, Finn look pissed, so perhaps he was growing a spine.

"I figured you would find out soon enough."

Finn scowled.

"Finn, you need to move on. Your obsession with Pop isn't healthy. At the rate you're going, you'll end up being a bachelor still pining after her while she celebrates her twenty-fifth wedding anniversary."

Finn flushed. "He's not good enough for her. He won't treat her as well as I will. Steve, you have to put a stop to it."

Steve shook his head. "You're being delusional, Finn. Richard is a perfectly nice man. Besides, Poppy is twenty-six and is quickly becoming an old maid. The sooner she gets married, the better. I don't want her to be alone. It's not good for a woman."

"I'll marry her!" Finn said almost desperately. "I'll give her a ring, build her a nice house, protect her and the children—"

"Are you proposing to me or her?" Steve cut him short. "I'm not going to force my sister to do anything, Finn. Either convince her to give you a chance, or let her go." His mood darkened. "And you'd better not try anything funny, like kidnapping her and dragging her to a church. Chris, I, and especially Hugh, will not stand for it."

Finn shook his head. "Of course not!"

Steve grasped his shoulder. "Good. Well then, Finn, I have something of utter importance which needs to be taken care of."

"What is it?" Ruby looked at the red-ribboned box with full-fledged curiosity. The box was white, with designs carved in pale blue paint in the form of flowers and swirls around it. It was heavy and looked expensive.

This was also the first time someone had given her a present without anything in return.

"A gift. Open it," Steve chided her gently. "You've been feeling so sad lately, a little gift might help."

Ruby seemed startled by the revelation as she gently pushed the box open as if afraid it was going to bite her. A blue ceramic bunny was next to a little white figurine of a woman wearing a blue dress. The bunny and the lady twirled in circles as a soft melody escaped from it.

The girl gaped as she closed the box and opened it, only to hear the music again.

Steve chuckled as he ran his thumb against her cheek. "It will continue playing. Do you like it, sweetling?"

She nodded, still staring at the box with adoration.

"Are you feeling better tonight?"

Ruby nodded, startled by the question. "Yes." She was still staring at the box. There was a weird expression on her face, not happiness exactly, but Steve could tell something was wrong.

He soon brushed the thoughts aside once Ruby gave him a peck on the cheek. Maybe she was still feeling a bit tired, but he made a mental note to ask Hugh to check up on her if she still felt sick.

Ruby peered up at him, with her big green eyes looking almost sorrowful. "Thank you."

Chapter 8

"IT LOOKS ALMOST DEMONIC, doesn't it, Ruby?"

A week later, a frightened Jeanette clutched Ruby's arm, the blonde starting to regret begging Jeanette to come. The girl was like a scared mouse. But she hadn't wanted to come alone, and Linda and Estella would just laugh at her misery. She certainly couldn't tell Steve, either. He would be furious.

Ruby placed a nervous hand on her belly. Once this was over, she doubted he would ever want to talk to her again. She hadn't been planning on telling him about the baby, but after he had given her the music box, the guilt had basically started to eat her alive.

Even their lovemaking this week, had been dull and robotic.

The baby was the size of a walnut, but she swore she could feel it kicking in protest. She was getting rid of a baby she didn't want. A baby who didn't deserve the life Ruby could give it, the life of a child born out of wedlock to the most expensive whore in town and the town sheriff.

"Don't be stupid," Ruby snapped as she looked to where Madame Eugenia had sent her. It was a shack in the outskirts of town, painted with faded green paint, with junk surrounding it.

An old, tattered sheet was hanging near the doorway amidst a broken sewing machine, old pots, and pans. She shivered; perhaps Jeanette wasn't far off. She had to do this, though. Madame Eugenia had sworn Mrs. Polling was the best healer in all of Larkspur Valley and that she would help her get rid of her "little problem".

"You'll be able to entertain men in your bed by the end of the week if everything goes well, girl," Madame Eugenia had promised.

Before she lost her bravery, Ruby arched her back, holding Jeanette strongly by the arm, forcing her inside the tiny shack.

The shack smelled of pork fat, as if someone had been butchering a pig. Ruby pressed a hand against her mouth, trying not to throw up. The morning sickness had been particularly terrible ever since she had found out she was pregnant. Any odd smell was enough to make her want to upchuck the little breakfast she was able to consume.

A hunched-up old woman was stirring something green, in a pot. Her hair was curly, wild, and gray. Her clothes were tattered and she was missing one front tooth. She looked like she belonged in a fairytale book.

"You must be Ruby," Mrs. Polling wheezed. "Eugenia told me you would come. Though she only mentioned one of you had a planted seed in your belly."

"Ruby is the one who's pregnant," Jeanette corrected. "I'm here for moral support."

"Madame Eugenia said you would be able to help me take care of this little problem."

Mrs. Polling gave her a toothy grin. "I will, girl, for fifty dollars."

Jeanette gasped.

Ruby didn't even blink as she carefully counted the money out of her little drawstring purse. Mrs. Polling snatched it away as soon as she offered it.

The blonde looked around, expecting to see saws or a large fork which would rip the baby out of her. She gulped, suddenly wishing Steve were here, because Jeanette looked like she was about to pass out.

"Do we do the surgery here?"

Mrs. Polling let out a loud laugh. "No surgery. You're barely two months."

"Three, next week."

"Either way, it is still in the early stages. My special tonic should do it." The old woman started serving the mixed substance in a large jar before handing it to her. "Drink this as soon as you get back to the brothel. The baby should slip out of you by breakfast."

"S-slip out?" She imagined little baby arms and reproachful looks staring back at her, accusing her of killing it and damning her to hell.

"It will just be blood. Your baby is the size of a peanut right now. You wouldn't be able to tell the difference between a head and an arm. It's a good thing you came to me when you did. Otherwise, I would have to open you up. A little slip of a girl like you would never make it out alive. Be a smart girl, take the tonic, and be done with it. Understood?"

She nodded. "Will it hurt?"

"Nothing more than a stomach ache."

Ruby and Jeanette didn't speak during the entire ride back to the brothel. Once she was inside her bedroom, she sat on her bed clutching the bottle. A hand was pressed to her belly as she gulped.

Guilt was practically causing her throat to close off. Her skin felt prickly and the tears were starting to form against her green eyes.

"I'm sorry, baby," she whispered. "But this world is cruel. It will destroy you. You will be better off without me as a mother."

Pressing the bottle against her lips, she swallowed the liquid in one gulp, feeling the burning sensation in her throat from whatever disgusting ingredients were inside destined to kill her baby. Ruby pressed a hand against her mouth to prevent herself from throwing up. She threw the bottle against the floor, breaking it. It was done.

The blonde woke up at two in the morning feeling violently ill. Her entire body shook, her skin had turned into a waxy, white color, and she could barely let out a word without her teeth chattering.

Most of all, her belly felt like it was on fire, and her organs felt like they were twisting inside her as if they wanted to kill her from the inside. The pain continued on until time to get up, growing more painful by the minute. She waited for the blood to show between her legs, but there wasn't any.

Ruby whimpered. How much longer?

Loud arguing was starting to come from downstairs, followed by loud foot stomps. She heard Madame Eugenia's flustered voice, "Mr. Bennington, you cannot come up here. It's improper. Ruby is ill, she needs her rest."

"If she is truly ill, then I need to see her. I will take her to my brother," Steve argued hotly.

Before she could even get up from where she was a sweaty, anxious mess on the floor of her bedroom, the door opened. Madame Eugenia looked annoyed at Steve, but he was ignoring her. Instead, he was looking straight at Ruby who surely must be looking like a corpse.

Ruby tried to protest that she was fine when she was greeted by another sharp pain in her upper stomach which reduced her to tears.

Steve immediately scooped her up in his arms. "Don't

worry, Ruby. I'm going to take you to Hugh. You'll be as right as rain soon, baby, I promise."

But then you'll hate me forever. Ruby buried her face inside his chest, her body relaxing. It was as if her body knew all along that what she had needed was Steve.

"Well, Miss Green, you're still pregnant. The powder I gave you should help with the stomach pains, but take it easy for a day or two. Soup will help, over heavier dishes like—"

"Excuse me, pregnant?" Steve interrupted, shock evident on his face. He looked between Ruby and his brother. Hugh had a nonchalant expression on his handsome face, but Ruby was too embarrassed to look him in the eye. "Ruby, look at me. Are you pregnant? Is it mine? Of course, it is, you haven't lain with anyone else in months."

Ruby ignored his questions as she looked nervously at Hugh. "The tonic the healer gave me was supposed to get rid of the baby."

Hugh shrugged. "From what you told me, her tonic was a combination of her herbs and dirty water. Perhaps some women get more violently sick and it causes them to lose the baby. Unfortunately, your child is stubborn, like its mother and father—"

It was the last thing Hugh said before Steve punched him across the mouth.

Chapter 9

"STOP IT! Stop it! You'll kill him!"

Steve heard Ruby's screams from behind him and felt her dig her little nails against his shoulder in a weak attempt to get him off his baby brother, whom he was currently beating to a bloody pulp.

"Steve!" she shrieked, sounding more girlish than he had ever heard her before.

"Stay out of this!" he growled at her, shrugging her off. For once, she kept her mouth shut and, instead, just scurried off to the corner of the room like a scared mouse.

He turned back to Hugh who was wiping off the blood which was trailing down his lip. Hugh didn't look the least bit upset. Instead, he was grinning at him like a sick bastard. The idiot had always loved violence. The only reason he hadn't been kicked out of medical school was because Christopher kept paying off the college whenever Hugh's play fights got a little out of control.

Steve took a step forward, viewing him with cold eyes. "You knew Ruby was pregnant and you didn't tell me?"

"I was trying to save you, you poor, lovesick bastard."

Hugh cocked his head to the side. "Did you really want to saddle yourself to a whore and have a bastard child?"

Something inside Steve snapped as he lunged towards his brother again, pushing him to the floor. Hugh dug his knee into his stomach, but Steve was too fueled by anger to feel any pain. Instead, he landed punch after punch across Hugh's pretty face. "Don't. Call. My. Child. A. Bastard!"

Hugh spit blood on his cheek then dug his fingers against his scalp, pulling on the dark tresses. He landed a punch against Steve's throat and he let out a moan. "If you're looking for an apology, you won't get it from me. Don't you understand what she was doing? She was trying to get rid of your precious child. So perhaps you should cut your losses and—"

Steve didn't let him continue as he gripped one of his wrists. "Can't be much of a doctor if you don't have a working hand, can you?"

"Get off me, you jackass!"

Somewhere in the clinic, Ruby was crying non-stop, but he had no patience for her tears. It would be a miracle if he didn't end up killing his brother and Ruby tonight.

Somebody pulled Steve off Hugh.

"What is going on? What is wrong with both of you?" Anthony had pulled them off each other. Despite his slimmer appearance, he was stronger than he looked, and currently, he looked completely confused. "I was moving in when I saw you two fighting."

Anthony has recently graduated from divinity school early and was going to be taking over the town's Presbyterian church. He had clearly been moving into the old pastor's home when he heard the screams.

Steve scoffed. "Ask him."

He then went over to Ruby and plucked her from where she was hiding behind a cabinet and placed her over his shoulder. Ruby squeaked but, thankfully, didn't protest as he carried her to his own house, which was only a five-minute journey from his brother's practice.

Ruby squirmed over Steve's shoulder but stopped when he slapped her bottom. Her stomach still hurt, but the only thing on her mind was that there was still a baby in her belly. A baby Steve now knew about and she would not be able to get rid of so easily.

Steve took her to his bedroom where he plopped her down on the bed. Ruby flinched when he pulled out a rope from his dresser and started tying her to the bed by her wrists. Ruby started flailing around like a chicken with her head cut off, but Steve was much too strong for her.

"Let me go, Steve," she whispered quietly. "Please."

"No." Steve gave a final knot before he kissed her firmly. "I will never let you go, Ruby. You're going to stay here with me. Marry me."

"No. I don't want to marry you and I don't want the baby," she whispered. "And I know you don't, either. This wasn't planned. Steve, help me get rid of the baby so the both of us can return to our own lives—"

"You don't know what I want," he interrupted coldly. "But this sneaking around, along with this absurd idea of you giving up the baby, stops now, young lady. Do you hear me?"

"You can't stop me! You can't force me to have a baby!" she spat angrily.

He looked at her darkly. "Watch me."

Then he closed the door.

A few days passed and neither Ruby nor Steve's mood improved. He left Ruby tied up in his bed when he was at work, coming by every few hours to feed her and let her relive herself. At night, he wrapped his arms tightly around her, refusing to let her go, like a stubborn bear.

Ruby had not taken to this well and he was often the

victim of cruel words and scratches against his cheek and neck. He didn't care. He had dealt with worse, and as long as Ruby was carrying their child in her belly, he wouldn't spank her.

Before Steve knew it, it was his sister-in-law Lucy's birthday, and after putting an angrily sobbing Ruby down for a nap, he made his way to his brother's house. But not even cake and celebration put him out of his sour mood. It didn't help that Hugh was completely unapologetic about hiding something as big as a pregnancy.

Finally, losing his patience, he found his way outside, punching a lone haystack, venting out his frustration until his knuckles bled. It was something his father had taught him and his brothers to do when they were angry. He suddenly wished he were here right now because he didn't know what the hell he was going to do with Ruby.

"What did that haystack do to you?"

Steve turned around and found Christopher staring at him with a raised eyebrow and crossing his arms over his chest. What was he doing here? He was supposed to be with his wife who was celebrating her birthday.

Steve gave him a sour expression. "What are you doing here?"

"Lucy sent me. She's worried about you."

"She doesn't have to be." He punched the haystack again, his knuckles bloody. Of course, his sweet sister-in-law had sent him, he and his brothers were as emotional as a piece of wood.

Christopher pulled him away, pushing him against the haystack so he couldn't hurt himself any more. He gripped Steve by the shoulder. "What's wrong? I cannot help you if you don't tell me."

Steve laughed humorlessly. "Can you take care of a pregnancy?"

Christopher pulled back. His shock was almost comical. "Pregnancy? Who's pregnant?"

Steve didn't say anything for a few minutes, but he had a somber expression on his face. "Ruby."

"Ruby?" Christopher frowned. "I didn't know you were courting anyone."

"I'm not," he said tightly. "Ruby is a fallen woman. She works at Madame Eugenia's whorehouse. I've been going to her for a few months. She's only nineteen." He shut his eyes. "She's three months pregnant, and the only reason the little chit finally squealed was because she was attempting to get rid of the baby."

"Would it have been so bad?" he asked lightly. "She's a soiled dove. You two will never be able to live peacefully in Larkspur Valley, perhaps it would be best—"

Steve's eyes became murderous as he pushed his brother. "Would you tell Lucy the same thing?"

"Of course not, but she's not pregnant. Besides, we're married," Christopher stated calmly. "You got this Ruby pregnant out of wedlock, and she's a fallen woman."

"Stop calling her that!"

"You know I'm right. Neither you, nor Ruby and the baby will have a happy life if she gives birth to the baby," Christopher announced calmly. "You should have been more careful. The way I see it, you have three options. You send Ruby away from Larkspur Valley so she has a chance at a decent life, she gets rid of the baby and there are medicine women who can help if that option is where Ruby seems to be headed, or you do the decent thing and marry the girl. The rumors and dirty looks will die off eventually, and you should be man enough to take it."

Steve ran a hand through his dark hair, sulking. "She doesn't want to get married. I already proposed. She wants to get rid of the baby and continue bedding strangers for a living."

Christopher took a deep breath, torn between wanting to comfort his brother and strangle him for being so stupid as to get a girl pregnant. "Is there anything I can do to help?"

Steve shook his head sadly. "No, I will take care of it. Go back and enjoy your wife's birthday. Give Lucy my apologies. I'm going to the saloon to get myself a much-needed drink."

"Steve, what kind of girl is Ruby?"

He shook his head. "A stubborn, arrogant little hellion who would argue with God if He stood before her. She can be sweet when she wants to be, which is rare. She's kind of like a cactus."

Christopher snorted. "Lucky man. I'll see you tomorrow."

Chapter 10

RUBY OPENED her mouth as Steve fed her a bit of egg with bacon. It had been a few days since he had locked her in his home, and he was still keeping her like a prisoner. When he was at work or visiting his family, he kept her tied by her legs to his bed. He stopped tying her by her arms when she started complaining that she got too sore.

When he was at home, he let her roam around, but he kept his distance. Still, his blue eyes were never far away from her, especially her belly. One couldn't tell, because of her bulky dresses, but underneath her clothes, her belly had rounded slightly.

It was the first time her belly wasn't flat with her ribs sticking out, though it was also the first time she had had enough to eat. She might be the sheriff's prisoner, but he didn't treat her cruelly even though she knew he was probably dying to belt her. It seemed he wouldn't spank her while pregnant and she was grateful for small miracles.

Currently, Steve had plopped Ruby on his lap and was feeding her breakfast. Since she had a tendency to stuff her mouth, she often ended up disposing of her breakfast shortly after. As a result, Steve had taken over feeding her, by giving her small spoonfuls of food while he sat her on his lap.

Their anger with each other had diminished somewhat and they managed to have decent, short conversations without biting each other's heads off, which was a feat in itself.

Once he finished feeding her, Ruby expected him to let her go so she could go back to her usual routine of pouting, but he didn't. Instead, he gripped her by the waist tighter, his fingers caressing her belly.

Ruby swallowed. Unlike her, it seemed Steve was excited to be a father and had already accepted the situation, while Ruby was still praying for a miscarriage. She didn't want a baby, but unfortunately for her, it seemed to fall on deaf ears. There was no way Steve would allow her to get rid of the baby, and at this point in her pregnancy, they would probably have to yank the baby out.

"We're getting married in three days." Steve announced calmly as if they were talking about the weather.

"What?" she shrieked. The young woman tried to get up from his lap, but he had a tight grip on her.

"Put on your shoes," Steve continued in his usual dry voice. "We are going to visit my family to tell them about the wedding. Anthony already knows, as he will marry us."

"I don't want to get married." The blonde scowled. "Did you even think about asking me if I wanted to marry you, you big oaf?"

The insult rolled off his back as he stood up. To Ruby, he now looked larger and more intimidating. "I'm afraid what you want became irrelevant the minute you became pregnant, Ruby. You are carrying my child; therefore, we will be getting married. I won't have my child be a bastard and grow up without a father figure or have you roaming around, being the town laughingstock. It goes without saying that you will quit your job at Madame Eugenia's, effective immediately."

Neither Madame Eugenia nor any of the girls had visited her, no doubt her new "fiancé" had scared them off.

"Steve, you don't want to marry me," Ruby stated desperately. "The pregnancy is still in the early stages. We can fix this, go to another healer who—"

Steve pressed her against the wall, his arms caging her in. Their faces were pressed so tightly together that if Ruby were leaning even slightly forward, they would be kissing.

"No," Steve said in a deadly calm tone. Ruby almost missed his anger. He sounded tired and defeated. "We made this mess, and now we have to own up to it and do the proper thing. Our child will not suffer."

"But you will have me suffer?" Ruby laughed coldly. She had never planned to marry, especially after how useless her own father had been. "I'm not the girl your family expects you to marry, Steve."

Steve didn't answer as he let her go. "Get your shoes and shawl. It is done."

When Ruby didn't move, he picked her up by the waist and dragged her to the wagon which, thankfully, already had the horses attached. Ruby's eyes burned with unfallen tears as she wiggled her stocking-covered feet. "I hate you," she whispered. "Even if we marry, I will still hate you."

A flash of pain crossed his face as he gripped the reins. "Hate me all you want. It's not going to change my mind."

They rode to Christopher and Lucy's house in silence. It was a beautiful two-story home and Lucy obviously kept it very tidy. Ruby dismissed Steve's attempt to help her as she jumped out of the wagon like a cat and stomped inside the house.

Ruby's bravado diminished when seven pairs of eyes stared back at her. Christopher Bennington was standing in the sitting room with his arms crossed, looking tense, as his wife, Lucy, passed out cookies.

Hugh was sitting down with his shirt half unbuttoned, obviously bored out of his mind, while Anthony looked around worriedly. The ones who seemed oblivious to what this meeting was for were Steve's unmarried sisters.

Poppy, the eldest, was finishing sewing the buttons on a dress. Iris was reading a large poetry book while Lily was grumbling about a homework piece she couldn't complete.

They all turned to stare at her when she barged in and she was suddenly aware of the fact she didn't have shoes on. Lucy was the only one who gave her a look filled with sympathy. She squeezed her arm as she led her inside. "Hello, Ruby. Come on in."

"Where are your shoes? Are you poor?" Lily commented curiously as Iris tugged on her braid in a scolding matter.

"No, I'm not." In fact, she had quite a tidy sum in the bank thanks to Steve's payments. "I just forgot them."

"Understandable, please sit." Lucy led her to a chair next to Poppy, who was eying her suspiciously. It was quite clear she and Hugh were fraternal twins—they both had that sharp look in their eyes, letting others know they weren't easily fooled. "Can I get you tea, coffee, cookies?"

"No, thank you," Ruby whispered, wanting to leave.

Steve placed a reassuring hand on her shoulder, clearing his throat as he looked at his siblings. "We'll make this quick. Everyone, this is Ruby Green. She's expecting my child and we are going to be married."

Iris started stuttering, trying to make sense of things, while Lily started squealing about how she was going to be an aunt. Poppy, however, narrowed her eyes at her like an angry cat. It was quite obvious that while Iris and Lily were oblivious about her "profession", Poppy knew everything.

"Was this your plan all along, Ruby?" Poppy demanded. "I know the type of girl you are; did you enchant Steve because you knew he had money? Is that even his baby?"

"Poppy!" All of the men glared at the blonde who did not look the least bit apologetic. Apparently, they were used to her outbursts and sharp tongue.

"Iris, take Lily upstairs," Hugh barked.

Iris looked annoyed at being sent away but did as she was told.

Steve gripped his sister's arm. "Apologize."

Poppy did no such thing.

"It's his baby," Ruby spat. "Do you honestly think I want to be a wife? Blame your brother if you're so against me being part of your precious family."

"Then I guess it was just a coincidence that you managed to get pregnant by the town sheriff?"

"Poppy, shut up!" Hugh snapped.

"Your brother was the one begging for me." Ruby cocked her head to the side. "Though I suppose you don't know how that feels, you horrid little spinster."

Poppy reddened.

Lucy laughed nervously as she tugged on a brown curl. "How about all of us calm down? A baby, Ruby, how exciting. Congratulations, Steve and Ruby, on your nuptials. We will be happy to help you with the wedding, won't we, Chris?"

Christopher kissed the top of his wife's head. "Of course, honey." He then glared at Poppy. "Pop, behave yourself. I won't have you at the wedding if you're going to behave like a brat."

Poppy snorted but didn't argue.

Steve was stiff beside her. "Well, we wanted to let you know of our plans. The wedding is set for three days from now."

When Steve and Anthony excused themselves to talk about the finishing touches for the wedding, Ruby quite swiftly managed to corner the eldest Bennington brother when he was refilling his cup of coffee.

"You need to get Steve to call off the wedding," Ruby begged him desperately.

Chris raised an eyebrow. "Why would I do that?"

"Because he listens to you. You're his big brother." Ruby clutched his shirt in her hands. "I know you don't want him marrying a whore. I won't be a good wife to him, or a good mother. This problem can be solved without marriage. Please, Christopher, help me convince him. This is not the life Steve deserves."

Christopher untangled himself from her. His words were firm, but his eyes were full of pity. "I can't convince Steve to do anything he doesn't want, and what he wants is marriage and a baby with you, Ruby. My fool of a brother is completely in love with you. He won't stop until you're Mrs. Bennington and he has his baby in his arms. I'm sorry this happened, Ruby, but I'm afraid my hands are tied."

Ruby watched as he left, taking what felt like her freedom with him.

Three days later, Ruby Green was standing in Larkspur Valley's Presbyterian Church, minutes away from being Mrs. Bennington. Madame Eugenia, Jeanette, Linda, and Estella were sitting in the back pew, looking prim and proper in matching gray dresses.

They hadn't said much to her but "good luck" and the blonde suddenly longed for the brothel.

Ruby suddenly felt suffocated in the blue dress Lucy had

let her borrow. The entire neckline of the dress was covered in fancy white lace which felt extremely itchy.

Iris was standing in front of her, but she didn't notice her meltdown because she was too busy fixing Lily's hat even though she was too old to be a flower girl.

Poppy had refused to participate in the wedding and was currently sulking next to Lucy on the front pew, along with Finn who was keeping an eye on her. Hugh was standing next to his brother, even though the bruises on his handsome face were still noticeable.

Ruby felt her heart jump inside her chest and the baby stir in her belly when she saw her future husband. Steve looked positively even more handsome today, on their wedding day, with his dark suit and his shining blue eyes.

The blonde suddenly felt guilty for being such a brat due to the wedding, but honestly, could anyone blame her? She had gone from being a whore to finding out she was pregnant to becoming Mrs. Bennington, all in a matter of days.

Not to mention, the stubborn Bennington was refusing to take no for an answer. Not that she could blame him, he was the baby's father after all. He came from a large, loving family so, of course, he would want to be involved.

"Ready?"

Ruby looked up and saw Christopher waiting for her. Since her daddy was dead and he was the only other Bennington sibling who was married, he was going to walk her down the aisle. He was offering his arm to her. Even though it was clear he didn't approve of the marriage, at least he wasn't being a jerk about it, like Poppy and Hugh.

She let out a nervous chuckle. "Is there a way out of this?"

Christopher gave her a sympathetic smile. "What do you think?" He paused. "I know my brother is angry right now,

Ruby, but he's a good man. He will make sure you and the baby are taken care of."

"I know he will," Ruby responded softly. "I'm just not sure we're right for each other."

Loud music started playing from the organ as Christopher took her arm gently. "Well, Miss Green, it's a little late for that."

Chapter 11

"OH! DAMN IT! DAMN!" Ruby hurried and grabbed the pan from the stove, hoping to save her eggs. She was unsuccessful and black eggs stared back at her, burnt to a crisp. She sadly dumped them in the trash along with her earlier attempts at making pancakes.

What was the point? She was a lousy housewife.

Ruby and Steve had been married for two weeks and she still couldn't get breakfast right. She had a feeling Steve was starting to regret being married to her because he would often leave before she woke up and return when she was getting ready for bed. Ruby doubted work was that exciting. More than likely, he was avoiding her and her terrible wife skills.

In the two short weeks, she had burned most of their meals, broken three plates and two glasses while washing dishes, burned two of Steve's Sunday suits with her iron, and had laundry piling everywhere.

Ruby sighed as she took off her apron. She needed to run to the mercantile and buy more food. They couldn't just rely on Lucy and Christopher's generous invitations to Sunday dinner. At this point, Ruby would rather be entertaining men at Madame Eugenia's than be a wife.

She hadn't seem Madame Eugenia or Linda, Estella, or Jeanette since Steve dragged her to his home. They had probably been ordered to stay away, and she couldn't believe she actually missed Estella and Linda's mocking.

Ruby grabbed a small basket for her purchases and headed out the door. Steve let her roam around town now, probably because she had his ring on her finger and her belly was growing larger by the day. Not to mention, Hugh and Anthony had probably been instructed to keep an eye on her.

The blonde wrapped her shawl around her shoulders, trying to ignore the curious glances of the townspeople. By now, everyone knew the sheriff had married his pregnant whore. They didn't talk to her as they talked to Lucy or the other Bennington girls; instead, they kept their distance. Ruby preferred that.

At the mercantile, she bought eggs, flour, tea, and a tin of cookies from Mr. Simon. If she managed to burn breakfast again, then at least she could get full on tea and cookies.

She was halfway home when she saw Steve outside the sheriff's office. He was talking to a pretty brunette who was wearing a blue and green bonnet with a ridiculous large bow under her chin. They were laughing together over something Steve had said. Steve was showing off his strong, white teeth.

Steve had never laughed that hard, especially since he found out Ruby was pregnant.

A flash of jealousy splashed through her as she continued watching them. When she couldn't stand it anymore, she ran home in a fit of rage, slamming the door behind herself.

Ruby sank to her knees, feeling as if she were going to cry. She and Steve should have never gotten married. It was clear they weren't right for each other. Steve should have been with the pretty brunette with the tasteful clothes and stellar reputation who didn't burn eggs.

The rest of the day was spent with Ruby angrily cleaning, feeling sorry for herself, and trying not to burst into Steve's office to kill him with her bare hands. Why would he insist on marrying her if he was just going to continue flirting with other women?

Steve came in through the door at half past five, whistling cheerfully.

"Honey, I'm home."

He was greeted by an angry-looking Ruby who started hitting him with the broom. "How dare you come in here and act like nothing is wrong? If you think you're going to make a fool out of me in front of the entire town, then you are mistaken."

"Ow, Ruby!" Steve snatched the broom away from her and then landed three sharp smacks on her bottom which caused her to yelp. "What the hell has gotten into you, you little brat?"

"You know what you did!" Ruby's eyes were wet with tears as she tried to rub the sting away from her bottom. "I saw you flirting with that woman!"

He blinked, confused. "What woman?"

"The one with the blue and green bonnet," she snarled, reaching back for the broom, but Steve landed another smack on her rear end. "Stop spanking me!"

"Then stop acting like a lunatic." He looked at her wryly, torn between amusement and exhaustion. "The woman's name is Heidi, and she's my deputy's wife. She brought us lunch. I was just being friendly. She's a married woman, Ruby, just like you. I have no interest in extramarital affairs." He squeezed her cheek. "Were you jealous, my little Ruby?"

She blushed, suddenly feeling like a fool. "No."

"Ruby."

"A little," she grudgingly admitted.

Steve seemed satisfied by her answer because he landed a soft kiss on her lips as a reward. "Thank you for your honesty." He then grinned at her like the silly man he was. "You have nothing to worry about, Ruby. I would never be with another woman. I made vows to you and I will keep them."

She looked up at him, her eyes vulnerable. "I'm sorry for hitting you with the broom," she whispered. "I thought that once you married me, you would lose interest in me."

He laughed. "Lose interest in you? Ruby, you are the most beautiful, most complicated headache I have ever come across." His fingers caressed her belly. "Besides, you are carrying our child, and that makes you the most important person in my life. I would never jeopardize our marriage."

"I'm pretty sure there was an insult in there somewhere," she grumbled, but her looks softened before she wrapped her arms around his waist.

Steve leaned down and kissed her, his large hands rubbing up and down her back. His kiss was warm, inviting and much nicer than the simple, chaste kiss he had given her during their wedding.

His fingers started undoing the buttons of her dress as she pressed her body against his, rubbing herself. It had been weeks since she'd had sex. She was starting to feel like a virgin again.

Steve cupped her breast in his hand, his growing cock rubbing against her belly. "Are you sure? Do you feel well enough?"

"I'm never too tired to be with you, Sheriff," she murmured as she cradled his full balls in her hand, caressing them through the thick cloth of his trousers. "Take me."

He didn't have to be told twice, as he finished unclothing her until she was once again naked as she so often was. Her peach-colored nipples perked up to the chilly air as he stared at her with lustful eyes.

Ruby's hands went towards his belt buckle, and with expert hands, she started removing the belt while he disposed of his shirt. His cock sprang free, making Ruby giggle with glee and anticipation.

Steve immediately pushed her in for a kiss, his hand running through her golden hair. "You're so beautiful, my Ruby," he murmured as he pressed her breasts against his muscled chest. "My beautiful wife."

"I'm starting to think that's the only reason you married me," she teased him slightly.

He shook his head seriously. "No. I know you're beautiful, Ruby, but you're more than your beauty."

"Like?" she questioned as her hand rubbed up and down his manhood, causing it to stir in her hand.

"You're strong, quite clever, as well. You are never truly afraid to give me a tongue-lashing when you feel I need it." A finger poked her cheek. "Few people have the strength to stand up to me. I wonder if it was wise to marry one who actually will."

Ruby giggled, obviously pleased by the compliment. "Fuck me, Steve."

For a second, she thought he was going to scold her for her unladylike words, but he simply grinned. "It will be my pleasure, wife."

He scooped her up in his arms, careful with her belly at all times. Ruby wrapped her legs around his waist, her wet slit rubbing against his lower stomach while she kissed him firmly. Her nails were running sharply up and down his back, marking him.

Steve placed her on their dining room table, spreading her legs firmly with his thighs so she was exposed. He whistled as he dipped his finger into her. "You're already aroused for me, honey." His eyes twinkled. "Did you miss me that much?"

An embarrassed growl escaped her lips as she tried to pull away, but he entered a second finger, then a third, until he was slowly fucking her with his fingers until she was a whimpering, wet mess.

Ruby needed more. She needed something bigger inside her.

She tried to reach for his cock, but her arms were too short and she just ended up squirming over the table.

Steve chuckled at her poor attempt as he pushed her hand away, removed his fingers, and pushed his cock inside her in one quick thrust. Ruby moaned at the sudden fullness as she started wiggling her hips in glee, getting used to his length again after weeks of no sex.

He fucked her slowly at first, before he started increasing his speed once he saw she was readily asking for more. His thumb rubbed against her pink clit lazily, causing her hips to buck wildly in excitement.

Ruby panted as she lifted her hips in needy excitement, meeting each of his powerful strokes, her legs wrapped around his buttocks as she pushed him farther inside her.

Her full breasts bounced as his thrusts became slower and his thumb rubbing against her clit began to move faster. She was close. She could almost taste it, and it was glorious.

"Come for me, sweetheart," Steve ordered briskly with one quick pinch to her nipple.

For once, she wasn't annoyed at his bossy nature and did as she was told. She allowed the wave of ecstasy to hit her body as she felt him finish inside her, his warm, thick seed spilling between her legs. No wonder he had got her pregnant in a matter of weeks.

Steve noticed her heavy panting and he chuckled.

"Relax, I will let you rest for a bit. You don't have to be ready for a second round so soon."

Ruby glared at him. "I have no problem keeping up with you. Once I am done with you, you will be the one begging for a rest."

Steve stroked her hair as Ruby laid her head on his chest. They were silent for a few minutes until he spoke up in a quiet voice. "Ruby, I know we have had our ups and downs and this baby was a surprise, but how would you feel about making this work?"

"This?"

"Marriage. Baby. Life. I think we owe it to our baby to at least try. What do you say, honey? I'm willing to try if you are."

Guilt settled in Ruby's chest. She was barely adjusting to being a wife and she wasn't sure she even liked it, so how was she supposed to adjust to being a mother and care for a baby when her own parents hadn't even been present?

Steve didn't understand. He'd had a good childhood, with loving, supportive parents. He didn't understand how hard this was for Ruby, how she didn't have a maternal bone in her body and how a part of her wanted to rip the baby out of her belly and continue her free life as a whore.

But when she looked at Steve's hopeful blue eyes, she found she couldn't do it. It was too painful to hurt him, so instead, she said, "Yes, Steve, let's try."

Steve kissed her. "That's my girl."

———

Ruby must have been the object of the Bennington's pity because Christopher dropped off Lucy every Monday for cooking lessons and companionship, since it was clear she was never going to make friends with any of the town ladies.

Thankfully, Lucy's calm demeaner made it easy for even the socially awkward Ruby to feel safe in her presence.

"One cup of sugar, dear, that's salt." Lucy immediately took the measuring cup from her and exchanged it.

Ruby blushed, feeling like a moron. "I'm sorry. I've never really cooked."

Growing up, she had mostly relied on poorly made biscuits and pieces of salt pork because they couldn't afford anything else. It was hard to adjust to having all of the ingredients at her disposal.

"Don't worry, you will be an expert in no time," Lucy assured her warmly, which was a complete lie. "You just need a little bit of practice."

"Thank you for helping me," Ruby said sincerely.

Lucy squeezed her shoulder. "What are sisters-in-law for? We're family, and we must make sure we take care of each other."

Chapter 12

"YES, that's her. The soiled dove Sheriff Bennington married. She's only nineteen, can you believe it? I'd bet my allowance she has lain in bed with every single man in this town."

"Do you see how she walks, swinging her hips like that? It's like she wants to seduce men."

"She's so beautiful. Why do you think God makes devious women so beautiful?"

"To tempt men. Beautiful women are only good for one thing, that's what my mama says."

Anthony had barely finished his sermon five minutes ago, but Ruby had been called a variation of whore at least six times by now. She suddenly hated that Steve had left her alone, even though he had just gone to congratulate Anthony on a job well done.

"Don't listen to them. They weren't very nice to me in the beginning, either."

Ruby turned around and looked at Lucy, who was holding the youngest Bennington's hand. Lucy's curly brown hair was tucked in neatly in a sky-blue hat, and Lily looked precious in a red and white gingham dress. She wondered if her own baby would have blonde hair.

Ruby blushed. "It doesn't bother me."

Lucy smiled at her, obviously not believing her. Ruby was tired of feeling like a charity case.

"They were mean to Lucy at first," Lily piped up, oblivious to the fact no one was in the mood for talking. "But Poppy threatened to beat them up, so they stopped. Everyone is scared of Poppy."

"It wouldn't surprise me if they were," she agreed wryly. Poppy didn't seem like the type to cower easily.

"What are you going to name your baby?" Lily pressed a hand against her belly. Ruby had started to feel her baby inside her, and just yesterday, she swore she felt a kick.

"Lily," Lucy chided her gently.

"It's okay," Ruby reassured her, trying to think of something. To be honest, neither she nor Steve had brought up the idea of baby names. It seemed they just wanted to get through this pregnancy in one piece first. "We haven't decided. I suppose we'll have to wait until we find out if it's a boy or girl before we start discussing names."

Lily smiled at her. "You should name them after a color since your name is Ruby, like Sapphire or Gray."

"I will certainly think about it."

Lucy removed Lily's hand away from Ruby's belly when she noticed the blonde was getting embarrassed from all the curious looks people were giving her. "Lily, come with me, we must congratulate your brother for his wonderful sermon. We'll see you later, Ruby."

Christopher and Lucy hosted a large dinner every Sunday evening, and Ruby and Steve always attended. Ruby was just glad she didn't have to cook.

Ruby waited for a few more painful minutes for her husband while pretending to read her Bible, ignoring the continued whispering. Finally, Steve appeared with his large hand wrapping around her waist.

"Will you be all right walking home by yourself? Hugh and I are staying to help Anthony move a few things."

She rolled her eyes. "It's five minutes away."

Steve patted her on her hip then her belly. He had gotten into the habit of doing that now, as if he were afraid the baby would just run away. "Just checking. Take a nap before dinner."

"Yes, sir," she responded sarcastically.

Steve gave her cheek a little pinch before leaving her. As soon as his back was turned, Ruby practically ran to the door, only to be met by her least lovable sister-in-law, Poppy. Poppy raised an eyebrow. "Can I talk to you?"

Ruby hesitated but finally agreed. "If this is going to be another insult, then I will—"

"It's not an insult. I wanted to," Poppy hesitated, her cheeks turning red, "apologize. I was less than kind when I first found out about your situation. I'm sorry."

"Did Steve force you to apologize?"

"Steve can't force me to do anything." Poppy waved her hand impatiently. "I just thought since the baby will be here soon, it wouldn't be good if we were not in a good place. I might have been too quick to judge you. We're family, so it might be best if we put the past behind us." She raised her chin proudly. "Agree?"

"Agree." Ruby breathed a sigh of relief. At least Poppy wouldn't be a problem anymore.

"Ruby?"

"Yes?"

"If any of those girls bother you, let me know and I will put them in their places. No one messes with my family."

"Believe me, Pop, I have heard worse. If anyone will take care of anyone, it will be me."

Poppy smiled, obviously impressed.

Ruby was halfway back to her house when she was stopped once again. This time, it was by a tall, regal woman with soft brown hair and expensive-looking clothes. The woman smiled at her. "Are you Ruby Green?"

"Ruby Bennington now," Ruby corrected, wondering who this woman was. Every other woman, with the exception of her new family, had been avoiding her like the plague.

The woman smiled tightly at her. "Of course, my name is Clara Horace. My husband owns the big feed store across town. I believe you two have met."

"I don't think so——"

"Of course, you have. His name is Todd, and I believe he spent an evening in your lovely bed."

Chapter 13

RUBY'S MOUTH opened in shock, and for once, she didn't know what to say. She hadn't known what she had been expecting, but it certainly had not been this. Especially since this woman, Mrs. Clara Horace, looked so serene.

Shouldn't she be dragging Ruby down by her hair for sleeping with her husband?

The blonde placed a protective hand against her belly, silently hoping Clara would take pity on her, because she wasn't sure she could fight her in her pregnant state.

"It was only one night, months ago," Ruby protested. *He wasn't very good.* "I was in a different profession at the time, Mrs. Horace. Rest assured, it will not happen again."

"I can see that." Clara glanced at her belly. "Congratulations on your nuptials. Do not fret, Mrs. Bennington, I did not come here to make a scene. Todd and I have been married for fifteen years. I know how much of a wandering eye men can have, even with a loyal wife. Your sheriff will be no different."

"Steve's not like that!" Ruby blurted out angrily.

Clara looked skeptical. "If you say so. I'm surprised you

married him at all. Rumor around town was he had to take you down to the altar kicking and screaming. Your little friend Jeanette told me you didn't want the baby at all. Quite the chatterbox."

Damn it, Jeanette. Her cheeks grew hot. "It was a rather rough beginning, but Steve and I are working on it. We are going to make it work, for our baby."

"But you shouldn't have taken on a role you weren't prepared to take," Clara cooed, looking at her pregnant belly. "The role of a wife and mother can be very draining. I wouldn't blame a young, pretty girl like yourself for not wanting anything to do with it. You were making quite a nice amount of money before you found yourself in this situation, were you not?"

Ruby stiffened as she thought about her old profession. She would be lying if she said she didn't miss making her own money, even if Steve was plenty generous. Her old money was still sitting at the bank and she refused to touch it unless it was for an emergency.

"Life changes." Ruby wanted to get away from this odd woman.

"I'm infertile," Clara suddenly blurted out. "Todd and I have been trying for fifteen years for a baby, and nothing. Now, I'm too old, but I never gave up on my dream of having a little one. We have plenty of money and, of course, parental love to shower a child with, but alas, no baby. Do you see where I'm headed, Mrs. Bennington?"

"I don't understand."

"A thousand dollars," Clara said softly, "is what I am willing to give you, Mrs. Bennington, for your baby. I guarantee I will give your child a wonderful life, full of opportunities, and with the money I am willing to give you, you will be able to leave Larkspur Valley and go where no one knows you. Start anew, go back to entertaining men, or start a business."

A thousand dollars was a lot of money. More than she had even seen before. She couldn't believe she was actually thinking about this. But she had told Steve from the start that she hadn't wanted to be a mother. She would be a terrible mother, actually, given her own upbringing. The child deserved better than two parents who were trying to "make it work".

"What about Steve?"

Clara shrugged unapologetically. "He's a man. They are as parental as a piece of wood. He's handsome, well off, and holds a powerful position in town. He will find another pretty young thing once you run off, he'll annual the marriage and have another baby. Before you know it, Ruby, you and this baby will be a thing of the past."

Ruby's throat hurt. She wasn't excited about being a mother, but she also didn't want Steve to marry someone else. Besides, how could she just give up her baby to this woman? "He'll know I gave you the baby."

"Not if I leave town the same day you give me the baby. I have a sister in Laramie, talk about her all the time, I could say she's sick and visit her for a spell. Then, after a few months, I can come back and tell them I adopted an abandoned baby from an orphanage. People do it all the time. Then both of us can have the life we always wanted." Clara pressed a hand against her shoulder. "Think about it, Ruby. Don't let your freedom escape you a second time. You are a beautiful girl. You can do anything you set your mind to."

Ruby suddenly saw her future flash in front of her, married to Steve, with half a dozen children because neither of them could keep their hands off each other, being spanked whenever she did something Steve didn't approve off. Steve could be sweet, but he could also be a strict disciplinarian.

With Steve and the baby at her side, she wouldn't be able to reach her dream and open her own brothel, be like Madame Eugenia, and have her own money. She would just be another Bennington wife, stuck in a town where no one liked her and everyone still saw her as a whore.

Clara was offering her a chance at freedom. She and her husband had plenty of money to make sure her child had a comfortable life. They had been trying for fifteen years to have a baby, so they obviously wanted a child. As for Steve, well, Clara was right. He was young and handsome. He would move on, hell, his siblings would probably be glad he wasn't married to a former prostitute anymore.

"I'll do it," she whispered, her stomach churning. "But we have to be discreet. It can't be right after the birth because Steve will be suspicious. I will need time to heal and the baby will need my milk."

Clara looked briefly annoyed but nodded. "Two months after the birth. Not a minute more. We will set up a time and place to exchange the money and the baby." She patted her cheek. "You're doing a good thing, Ruby."

When Ruby got home, she didn't nap. Instead, she was filled with nerves as she cleaned the house from top to bottom. She gripped her broom in her hand. Was she doing the right thing? Was she being horribly selfish? Of course, she was. If Steve found out what she was doing behind his back, he would kill her and never forgive her.

But then Ruby thought about her own freedom and dreams. She had never wanted to depend on a man, even one as wonderful as Steve. Ruby would never be independent saddled with a baby. There was no way in hell Steve would allow her to work or open a brothel, even after she gave birth. He was a traditional man and he would expect her to be at home.

Yes, it was a selfish decision, she decided as she swept, but it was the right one. This baby needed both parents who loved it, not an indecisive mother and a father who was trying to make it work.

"Honey, I'm home!" Steve came whistling in. He kissed the tip of her nose. "What are you doing? I told you to nap."

"I wasn't tired," Ruby replied softly as she let go of the broom and sank to her knees.

He looked surprised as he patted her shoulder. "You don't have to." She had been feeling nauseous lately and hadn't wanted to pleasure him in this way.

She shook her head. "I want to." This man was going to lose her and his baby in a matter of months. Pleasuring him with her mouth, was the least she could do.

Ruby pulled down his trousers so his cock sprang free. It was already red and swollen with need. She opened her mouth to let his cock in. It was warm and slippery inside her mouth, a mixture of salty and sweet.

She sucked on his manhood as he groaned in pleasure, running his fingers down her blonde hair. "A little harder, sweetheart."

Ruby did as she was told, sucking harder, making sure she got every inch of him even though she was choking a bit at the end. Her tongue swirled up and down his length, getting every inch of the pulsing organ currently residing inside her mouth. Her husband pumped his cock into her, always keeping an eye on her in case she needed to stop or needed a break.

When she circled her lips against his tip, she looked up at him with big blue eyes. Steve looked pained as he tried to hold his orgasm in. "Are you sure?" he asked.

Ruby nodded.

Steve came inside her, filling her mouth with his cum, and Ruby swallowed every last drop.

Steve cupped her chin in his hand. "Thank you. Would you like to have your turn?"

Ruby shook her head as she wiped the leftover cum from the corner of her lips. "I'm tired." Steve helped her up and placed a gentle kiss on her forehead.

Ruby felt her entire body burn.

She was a traitor.

***

Ruby entered her fifth month of pregnancy quietly, with Iris by her side. Steve seemed to have picked up that she was lonely at the house since she was a social pariah and it wouldn't be appropriate for her to spend time with her old friends at the brothel.

As a result, he often came for her around lunchtime, to drop her off at his sisters' house, the second Bennington home, where the three unmarried Bennington sisters lived. Since Lucy lived farther away from town, back at the larger ranch, it was closer.

She would mostly spend time with Iris since her calm presence was welcoming. While Poppy seemed to have made peace, she was about as welcoming as a porcupine, and Lily was too much and preferred to run around in the fields.

"What do you think?"

Ruby looked up and saw Iris holding a pair of yellow and white baby booties. "Who are those for?"

"For you, silly. Well, for the baby. I decided to do yellow since we don't know if it will be a girl or a boy. I know they're a little big, but babies grow so fast."

Ruby felt her heart sink. Iris' efforts would go to waste.

The baby would never wear them. "They're very nice. Thank you... ow!"

Iris shot up, looking at her with alarm. "What's wrong? Should I get Hugh?"

"No, I'm fine. The baby kicked me, ow, they did it again now." Ruby pressed a hand against her belly, feeling her child kick her harshly, letting her know it was there.

Iris looked relieved. "Is this the first time?"

She nodded. "It's moved a bit, but this is the first time it's kicked so hard. That's why I was startled. Would you like to touch?"

Iris hesitated before she nodded shyly, pressing a hand against Ruby's belly. The baby kicked once again, causing Iris to jump. She let out a nervous giggle. "Wow, it feels funny, but also nice. You have a little rancher in there. I can't wait to meet him or her."

The door opened and Steve came inside. She hadn't realized how late it was. He raised an eyebrow. "Is everything all right?"

"The baby kicked!" Iris let out an excited giggle. "Oh, Steve, it's so wonderful."

Steve smiled. "Really?" He pressed his large palm against her swollen belly. The baby kicked happily, recognizing its father. "Strong boy."

"It could be a girl," Ruby pointed out.

"Strong girl, just like her mother." Steve pressed a kiss against her forehead. "Let's go."

After saying goodbye to Iris, Steve helped his wife inside the wagon. She frowned when she didn't recognize the way they were going. "Are we going someplace else?"

"The lake." Steve stopped whistling. "It's not far from Chris' ranch. Father used to take us a lot when we were kids. Thought I should take you to see it."

Twenty minutes later, they found themselves at a beautiful lake surrounded by larkspur flowers.

"It's so pretty." Ruby grasped Steve by the shoulders as he helped her down. "How come you've never taken me here before?"

"It barely started getting warm, and truth be told, I haven't been here since my mother died."

Ruby noticed his pained expression. "I'm sorry."

"Don't be, she died a long time ago, and in return, we got Lily."

Steve placed a blanket on the ground as both of them settled in the center, cuddling with each other while they stared at the lake.

"I wish I could swim," she stated enviously.

"Next year, when you're not pregnant. The lake is deeper than it looks. I don't want you to get hurt."

I won't be here next year. "Steve," she clutched his shirt in her hand, "are you worried about becoming a father? Do you sometimes feel you won't be a good parent?"

Steve didn't speak for a moment. "Sometimes, but parenting is a learning process. We won't be perfect, but there is no such things are perfect parents. All I know is we will both love our child very much. My mother died when I was still a teenager, but she was a lovely woman, from what I remember. My father changed a lot when he lost my mother, but he was a good man. I learned a lot from him." He kissed her knuckles. "I swear to you, Ruby Bennington, I will try my hardest to be the best husband and father to you and our baby. Are you worried about being a mother?"

"A little," she confessed. "My father was a drunk. He died because he couldn't let go of the bottle, and my mother, she was a prostitute too. It was all she knew to do and it got her killed. I didn't have any role models like you did, Steve. I didn't come from a good family. I don't know the first thing about being a mother."

"It's okay to be nervous." Steve squeezed her shoulder, pulling her close. "Ruby, I know you will be a wonderful mother, even if you had a rough childhood."

"How do you know?"

"Because you are already thinking about our child's well-being." He tweaked her nose playfully. "Besides, you'll have me and my siblings to help you with anything you need. We're family now."

"Family." The word sounded foreign on her tongue.

He kissed her softly, unaware of her betrayal. "Family forever."

Chapter 14

FOUR MONTHS LATER...

"Ow! Ow! It hurts! Take it out!" Hot tears ran down Ruby's cheeks as she clutched the pillows at her side. She was surprised she hadn't ripped them open. Her nightgown was covered with sweat and her blonde bangs stuck to her forehead. "It hurts! Please take the baby out!"

She had been in labor for sixteen hours, the pain getting worse with each passing hour. It certainly didn't help that her brother-in-law, Hugh, was currently buried between her spread legs, tracking down the process.

"I want Steve," Ruby whimpered, surprised at her own admission. Steve had left her in the early hours of the morning when the contractions started, to send for the midwife. She had heard him four hours earlier when the midwife had hissed through the door that the baby would be coming soon and to send for the doctor.

That had been four hours ago and still no baby.

"Steve can't be here right now, sweetheart, you know that." Lucy looked apologetic as she started wiping her brow. Lucy had been with her since the pains had started, and as much as she was grateful for her, Ruby really wanted her husband. "It will be over before you know it and you'll have a beautiful baby."

"It hurts."

"I know, honey. I'm sorry."

"Ruby," Hugh barked. He had the bedside manner of a wasp. "I see the head. Three pushes should do it. I need you to stop crying and push."

Lucy gripped her hand. "Squeeze as hard as you want."

"Push!"

Ruby did as she was told, feeling her legs shake. It felt like her entire body below her waist was being ripped apart.

"Again."

Ruby clenched her teeth and did as she was told.

"Once more, Ruby."

Ruby gave one final push, lying her head back on the pillows, exhausted. She was going to kill Steve for getting her pregnant in the first place once she was feeling up to it.

Lucy kissed her cheek. "Oh, you did it, Ruby. The baby is just lovely."

She had been so exhausted, she had hardly noticed a baby crying loudly. A baby. Her baby was just a few feet away. Her eyes welled up with tears.

The midwife had started cleaning her up while Hugh cut the cord and started checking on the baby.

"Hugh," she squeaked. "How is it? Is the baby okay?"

"Ten fingers, ten toes, and a cry that can wake the dead." For the first time since she had known him, Hugh smiled like a proud uncle. "Congratulations, Ruby, you and my brother have a healthy baby girl."

A girl. The baby was a girl. A darling, sweet, innocent little girl. Not a damaged girl like Ruby, but a pure, good-hearted baby girl.

Hugh placed her daughter, wrapped in a yellow blanket

Lily and Iris had knitted for her, in Ruby's arms. A red-faced, pink thing with blonde hair and angry-looking blue eyes stared back at her, obviously not happy at being disturbed.

Maybe Steve was right, and their little girl would have her personality. The baby uncurled her hand from beneath the blanket and reached it towards her.

Ruby let out a choked sob as she touched her finger. "Hi, baby, I'm your mama."

The baby gurgled in response.

Ruby hugged her close to her chest. How could she have ever thought about giving her up? She might not be the best mother in the world, but she would certainly try her hardest. She'd had her daughter for five minutes and she couldn't imagine spending even one minute away from her. She would just have to talk to Clara and tell her the deal was off. The woman would have to find another baby.

Lucy kissed her cheek. "I'll get Steve. Congratulations, Ruby, she's beautiful."

"Thank you, Lucy, for being here."

When Steve came in, the midwife and Hugh left, with Hugh warning him that Ruby needed rest. Maybe he was starting to soften up.

Steve looked like a mess, with his rumpled clothes, tousled hair, and stubble. It was clear Christopher and Finn had given him alcohol to calm his nerves, because he kept stumbling around.

Steve kissed the top of her head. "She's beautiful, Ruby, like a little princess. How are you feeling?"

"Tired. Sore. Are you drunk?"

"Chris might have given me one too many whiskeys to prevent me from barging in. I'll sober up," he promised. He stared at the baby. "She has your blonde hair and your angry face."

She scowled. "And your blue eyes and love for making me suffer."

Steve laughed. "Have you thought about a name? You should name her, you were in labor more than half a day. Are you going with what Lily said and picking the name of a color?"

"Sort of," Ruby agreed softly. "I was thinking of Silver as her first name and Petunia as her middle name, for your mother."

Steve looked at her with a proud look on his face. "Silver Petunia Bennington. It has a nice ring to it."

The weeks passed rapidly and Ruby found herself falling more and more in love with her daughter. The sweet, apple-cheeked blonde baby would look at her with her big blue eyes as if Ruby were the most marvelous person on earth.

How could she have ever thought about giving her away because she had wanted to shed her responsibilities of being a mother?

Now, she couldn't imagine her life without Silver. All the pain of the birth and the aftermath had been worth it every time she held the sweet little bundle in her arms.

Silver was such a good, pretty baby who nursed when Ruby offered her breast and who seemed content lying in her crib watching her mother do housework. Silver made Ruby want to have half a dozen babies with Steve.

Baby Silver also had her father wrapped around her little finger. Steve absolutely adored his little girl. He would always wake Silver up with kisses and he would rush home from work to be with her and Ruby.

Both of them had been scared about being parents, and

while Ruby was no expert, she didn't think they were doing a bad job.

Ruby and the baby were showered with gifts, not just by Steve, but by the entire Bennington clan, since Silver was the first niece. Lily, Iris, and Lucy constantly knitted her little booties, mittens, and dresses. Even Hugh and Poppy had softened towards Silver, even though they had been against the marriage in the first place.

Linda, Estella, and Jeanette had paid a visit, bringing a small music box for Silver. Their visit was bittersweet, and even though she missed them somewhat, Ruby also knew their lives were too different now to continue the relationship they once had.

Ruby had managed to send an anonymous letter to Clara, telling her the deal was off and she was keeping her baby. However, Ruby had not heard back and she wasn't sure if it was good or bad.

Clara hadn't come to visit her, and she and Steve hadn't gone to church in a few weeks because she was healing from the birth. With any luck, Clara had already forgotten about her. It had been a stupid idea, anyway.

"There you go, darling," Ruby cooed in a surprisingly gentle voice as she settled Silver in the baby carriage Silver's Uncle Chris and Aunt Lucy had given her as a gift. Silver fussed a bit but calmed down when her mother handed her a stuffed rabbit Hugh had given her.

Ruby made her way down Main Street. She was heading to the church to talk to Anthony about a day for the christening. The day was still warm, though Ruby knew fall would soon approach. She worried about Silver; what if it got too cold for her? What if she got sick? She shook her head. Fussing wouldn't solve anything.

She was almost to the church when she felt someone grip

her arm. Her blood froze when she caught a better glance at who was pulling her arm. Clara.

Clara looked worse for wear, in a faded yellow dress, and there were dark circles under her eyes. She had a hungry, desperate look in her eyes as if she wanted to eat Ruby whole.

She shifted towards Silver, who was chewing on the stuffed toy's ear, and her gaze softened. "Is this my Sara? She's beautiful!"

Dread settled in Ruby's stomach. Clara still thought she was going to give up the baby. "This is not Sara," she said quickly. "This is Silver. Silver Bennington."

There was no recognition in Clara's face. People were starting to look, the curious glances having grown once news traveled about Silver. Apparently, they had been expecting her precious daughter to have been born with horns and a tail because she had been conceived out of wedlock.

"Clara, let's talk over here. It will be a bit more private." Ruby practically dragged Clara to the back of the feed store where they wouldn't be disturbed. The last thing she needed was for people to overhear their conversation and go blabbing back to Steve.

"She looks just like you except for her eyes." Clara continued to look at the baby. "Sara will be a real beauty, just like you. I'm glad. I wasn't a very pretty girl and life is always kinder to pretty girls."

"Her name is not Sara, it's Silver. While Silver might be beautiful, it is not the only way to define her." Ruby's voice was on edge. "Clara, did you not received my letter about our agreement?"

Clara's eyes bored into hers. "I received it."

"And?"

"I chose to ignore it. We made an agreement, Mrs. Bennington, and it would be rude if you broke it." She looked at Silver again, who giggled, unaware that the two women were fighting for her. "It's fortunate you are alone. Now, let me take the baby and—"

"She's not your baby, she's mine, and I will not let you have her!" Ruby snarled as she pulled the baby carriage back. The sudden movement caused Silver to start howling.

Clara glared at her. "Look at what you did. You made Sara cry."

"I'm trying to get her away from an insane woman, and stop calling her Sara!" Ruby snapped.

"You didn't even want her. Now is not the time to act maternal."

"I made a mistake. I should never had made a deal with you."

"But you did, and now it's time to pay up." Clara pulled on the front of the baby carriage, causing the baby to cry harder. "Why, a whore cannot be a good mother."

"If you say one more word about my mothering skills, I will scratch your eyeballs out."

"Give her to me, Ruby, a deal is a deal." Clara tried to pounce towards her, but Ruby moved away, dragging the carriage with her. Silver started crying.

"Get away from me, Clara, or I will make sure my husband puts you behind bars."

"Do you think your husband will be sympathetic to you once he finds out you tried to give his daughter away?"

A sharp slap stung her cheek as Ruby clutched it in her hand.

"What on earth is going on here? Why are you two fighting?"

Both women turned around and saw Christopher, Steve, and Todd standing behind them with confused faces. Ruby could hardly believe she had slept with Todd at one point.

Ruby's stomach suddenly felt heavy, and looking at Steve's sweet, confused face was not helping. "Nothing."

Steve wasn't buying it, though, and he took a step forward. There was a rare, serious expression on his face. "What did Clara mean about giving our daughter away?"

Damn it, he had heard the last part of the conversation. "Nothing, Steve. The woman is insane."

"I am not." Clara placed a hand on her chest, deeply offended as she wrapped her arm around her husband. "Todd, darling, this is the Ruby I was talking to you about. She was the one who was going to give us her baby. We'll finally have Sara, darling."

Todd choked on his spit. "What are you talking about, Clara?"

Steve approached his wife, a dark expression on his face. "Yes, what is Todd's wife talking about, Ruby?"

"What are you doing here, Steve?"

"Finn is sick, my brother needed help with the food for the animals. Now, answer my question, Ruby."

Sensing the tension, Christopher cleared his throat as he took the baby carriage. "Lucy is picking a new dress at the dressmaker. I'm sure she will love to see Silver. I'll let you four talk."

Steve didn't acknowledge his brother; instead, he gripped Ruby's shoulder. "Answer me, damn it. Ruby, what did Clara mean about you giving up the baby?"

"She didn't want the baby," Clara shrieked excitedly. "Ruby was going to give her to me and Todd in exchange for money so we could finally have a family. Ruby was going to use the money I gave her to start a new life."

The air was tense as Steve looked at her coldly. "Is this true?"

Ruby's voice shook and she was afraid she was going to faint. "It's not how it sounds. I was still pregnant when Clara and I talked. I was afraid about being a mother and wife. I'm sorry, Steve. I love Silver now. I would never—" Ruby reached for his hand, but he pulled away.

Steve threw a disgusted look at Todd; he had hated the man ever since he found out he slept with Ruby. "Did you know about this?"

"N-no," Todd stuttered. "I would never agree to such a stupid plan, kidnap Silver Bennington? I would rather bite my tongue off."

"She's not a Bennington, she's Sara," Clara tried to argue.

Todd shushed his wife. "I swear to you, Sheriff, I knew nothing of this. Clara, my wife, she's not well. The Lord has taken our children before we could meet them one too many times. Please forgive her."

Steve gave him a curt nod. "Do not let your wife near my wife again."

Todd nodded as he pushed his wife into the feed store, leaving the couple alone.

Ruby lowered her head. "Please, let me explain."

Steve let out a harsh laugh. "I got the story. You planned to give our innocent daughter away because you couldn't stand being a wife and mother. I'm to blame, I suppose. Everyone warned me I shouldn't have married you and I should have listened."

His words stung. "I made a mistake. You and Silver are the best thing I have in this life."

"Save your lies." Steve clutched her arm. "Let's go."

Chapter 15

RUBY PACED BACK and forth in the dirty jail cell. She didn't know how long she did it, it just felt like eternity. She had never gone to visit the jail. When she visited Steve, it was usually in his office.

Now, she knew why he never brought her over here. It was dirty, cramped, and smelled disgustingly like urine. Thankfully, it was empty. The townspeople did not need to know that the sheriff had locked her up because she was a terrible wife and mother.

She grabbed her swollen cheek which Clara had slapped. It was still practically sizzling and she wouldn't be surprised if the woman had left a mark. But she didn't care if she got beaten black and blue, as long as she had her daughter back.

Ruby felt her eyes well up with tears, but she refused to let them fall. As her good-for-nothing daddy always said, crying never solved anything. Besides, she needed to be in her right mind. She could be a crying mess once she got her daughter back.

The blonde wanted to strangle her past self for even

agreeing to give her baby to Clara. She should have known the woman was a nutcase.

Ruby stopped pacing when she heard the door open. She gripped the bars, not caring if they hadn't been washed in years. Her heart fell in disappointment when she saw her husband coming with a frown on his face. He didn't have the baby with him, not that she was surprised. A jail cell was no place for a baby.

However, he did have something else in his hand. A thick, brown leather strap. She shivered, thinking back to when he had first spanked her, how she had cried and begged for mercy as he had dished out punishment.

Steve had been lenient so far, but now that the pregnancy was over and she had willingly put their daughter in danger, it seemed he wasn't quite as forgiving. Even though she knew she deserved to be strapped, her legs quivered in fear.

"Where's the baby?" she asked quietly.

"With Lucy and Christopher." Steve's jaw clenched. She was surprised he hadn't broken it by how hard he was clenching his teeth. "I don't trust you with the baby."

His words hurt, but she couldn't blame him. She had willingly deceived him and planned to give their baby away to a complete stranger, the wife of a former client. Even if she had regretted her decision at the end, she had still done it and she couldn't take it back.

She hated the pain she had caused Steve, especially since he had been so gentle and lovable to her when she had rejected him at every passing turn before they had decided on a truce. Steve was looking at her with eyes full of betrayal, eyes that told her he would probably drown her in a river if he could.

"Please, Steve, I want to see our daughter."

"*My* daughter is perfectly safe with my brother and Lucy. Silver is an innocent. She shouldn't have to witness her parents fighting because her mother was planning on giving her away."

Her heart fell at the harshness of his words no matter how true they were. She gripped the bars, trying to pull on them, but of course, it was all for naught. "It was a mistake. I'm sorry. I was scared I didn't think I wanted to be a wife and mother, but I was—"

"Save your excuses," he snapped. "If you wanted to leave me, that's fine, I would find a way to forget you, but how do you abandon Silver? How in the hell did you carry my daughter for nine months and decide you would just simply give her away as if she were an old dress?"

"*Our* daughter," she corrected quietly. "And I told you it was a mistake. One I bitterly regret. The moment I saw Silver, she became my whole world. Please, Steve, don't keep her away from me. Please give me a second chance."

"Why should I? You've shown me time and time again that I do not know you, that you do not want me." He gave her a cold smile. "I should have never gotten involved with you. I fell in love with your beauty. I should have realized the selfish woman who roamed underneath."

Ruby didn't comment, but she felt her eyes well up with tears. Steve had every right to be angry and if he wanted to be cruel to her to feel better, so be it. She cleared her throat. "Please let me see Silver. She's still so little." He didn't look convinced. "I'm still breastfeeding her, Steve."

Her breasts felt heavy and sore with milk, reminding her that Silver had not been fed. She was probably screaming Lucy and Chris' house down.

"Fine," Steve said after a while. "I'll take you to her once we are done here. But be warned, Ruby, I am not letting you or Silver out of my sight again. I don't trust her with you."

She nodded, then her voice grew soft as she let out a

confession which had been inside her for a while now. "I love you, Steve."

He had been the first person she had told those words to. In the past, she had never allowed herself to be so vulnerable. Now, she feared she might be too late.

Steve didn't react, his jaw just tensed as if he was trying very hard not to strangle her. He ignored her confession, which only made Ruby's eyes well up with tears again. "We will continue to be married. We made vows, but rest assured, Mrs. Bennington, our marriage will be in name only. The relationship we had in the past is dead and buried. I hope you know that."

Ruby didn't answer, she simply looked at the floor.

Steve opened the jail cell door and gripped her arm, pulling her out. "You're getting a strapping and consider yourself lucky."

If this was any other situation, she would have fought with him or, at the very least, struggled a bit more. However, given the situation, she didn't. Ruby had earned this spanking. She had put their daughter in danger, and now she must pay the price.

Steve dragged her to a wooden desk which was covered in black ink and chipped in some places. He pushed her down with surprising gentleness, a hand resting on her lower back. "Keep your hands away," he ordered gruffly. "The last thing I want to do is harm anywhere else but your bottom."

Ruby was too busy trembling to answer, so she simply nodded. She felt as Steve roughly raised her skirts and pulled down her underthings—she was surprised he hadn't ripped them.

Her bottom was introduced to the chilly jail air though she knew it wasn't going to remain cold for long.

He placed the thick strap against her sensitive bottom cheeks, then she felt the heavy, leather spanking tool rub against her sensitive nates. She shut her eyes, her pride getting the best of her. Ruby would not allow herself to cry.

She had cried once during a spanking; it would not happen again.

The strap was removed from her bottom and she closed her eyes, bracing for the spanking. The first slap landed in the center of her cheeks with a loud slap.

A gasp escaped from Ruby when she felt the sharp sting left behind. She had barely gotten used to the first lick when the second one landed, then the third and the fourth, across the backs of her thighs.

Tears were falling with the stinging left behind. Her entire lower body was sore, feeling like it had swollen to twice its size, and she had no idea how much longer Steve would keep going.

The strapping continued, the leather landing harder with each smack until she was sure she couldn't feel her bottom anymore. How did Steve manage to spank her so hard?

Her cheeks jiggled every time the implement fell. Despite the harshness of the spanking, she wasn't blind to the wetness pooling between her legs as Steve turned her bottom bright red.

When he landed the strap against her rear end for the twentieth time, Ruby finally cried out. The tears were falling down her cheeks. "Please stop! I'm sorry!"

It was the first time she had spoken, and much to her surprise, Steve did stop. Ruby took the opportunity to look over her shoulder at her punished ass. Her poor little cheeks were as red as little ripe cherries. Just by looking at them, she knew sitting was going to be a problem.

Her fingertips rubbed across the sore globes and she whimpered at the pain. Her finger felt the small welts left behind by the strap which would cause her to burst into tears every time she moved. Steve had taught her a lesson indeed.

"Three more, Ruby," Steve announced coldly.

Ruby whimpered but removed her hand as she turned her face back to the wall. Steve seemed impressed by her response because he ran a hand through her blonde hair in a rare moment of affection.

The strap fell in quick succession three times, against the center of her cheeks, her butt bouncing in an almost lewd manner as she arched her hips forward as if willingly meeting the strap. Her legs pulled apart unknowingly, exposing her pussy as she buried her head in her hands as she cried. Not even her engorged clit rubbing against the table's edge, was enough to stop her from crying.

Why did her whole body get turned on because of a spanking when she felt her ass was on fire?

The young woman felt out of breath as she struggled and failed to hold on to the desk. Even though her husband had stopped spanking her, the stinging was still fresh on her sensitive skin.

She was out of breath and she struggled to say anything because she was crying so hard. Steve didn't comfort her even when he told her that her punishment was over and she had buried her face against his chest.

He was a cold statue.

"Let's go." Without a look back at her, he exited the jail, expecting her to follow him.

"I'm sorry," Ruby whispered at his retreating back.

Chapter 16

RUBY FOUND herself living in the second Bennington home under the watchful eye of Iris, Lily, and Poppy. Steve could barely stand the sight of her, but since he was at work for most of the day, he wanted somebody to keep a careful eye on Ruby and Silver.

When he informed her of this, she didn't complain. She would live in a well if it meant she would have her baby close to her.

His coldness, however, continued as the days passed, which hurt Ruby more than she would ever admit. She would have gladly taken another strapping if Steve would look at her without the look of disgust on his face.

He would come like clockwork after work, pick up the baby, and spend the rest of the evening cuddling with her and speaking to his sisters while ignoring his wife. He would then return to their home, leaving Ruby sharing a bedroom with twelve-year-old Lily. Because she was so used to Steve being next to her side, she hated being alone now.

Thankfully, Steve's sisters did not seem to feel the hatred their brother felt towards her. In fact, they almost felt sorry for her which she hadn't been expecting, especially from Poppy. She had tried to give away their niece after all.

"This will pass," Iris tried to reassure her as she sat across from her knitting Silver another baby blanket.

"I doubt it," Ruby grumbled as Silver slept at her breast after she had finished nursing. It had been three weeks since the incident and Steve still barely looked at her.

"What did you expect?" Poppy stopped washing dishes to stare at her. "You tried giving up your baby. Of course, Steve was going to be mad."

"But she felt bad afterwards," Lily squeaked as she held the dish towel firmly in her hand. Poor Lily, she was too sweet for this cruel world. She hoped Silver would grow up to be like her. Lord knew the world needed more Lilys instead of Rubys.

"It doesn't matter. She thought about it, and that's what Steve is mad about, even if she wasn't planning on going through with it." Poppy placed a hand on her hip.

"Thanks, Pop, for your honesty," Ruby groaned. This wasn't getting her anywhere.

Poppy shrugged, not offended by her blunt words.

Iris and Lily tried to distract Ruby by telling her about the Christmas festival their school was putting on in a few months. But the thought of Christmas only depressed Ruby more. Would Ruby and Steve each spend Christmas alone? It was their first one together. But what about the baby?

Her thoughts were interrupted when the door flew open and Anthony and Steve came in. Poppy immediately greeted Anthony and started fussing over him. She had practically raised Anthony, Iris, and Lily after their mother died and constantly fussed over them.

Steve approached her and Ruby found herself blushing like a schoolgirl as she saw her husband. It was funny, when they had first met, she couldn't stand him, and now she longed for his touch. Or at the very least, she wished he wouldn't look at her with such disgust.

He didn't smile at her or address her in any way. He simply took the sleeping baby from her. Silver wiggled in her sleep before she settled on her father's chest.

"Hello, sweetling."

As much as she loved how Steve treated their daughter, she missed when he addressed her like that. Ruby didn't know how much longer she could apologize, the words felt like sawdust in her mouth. Besides, Steve hardly paid any attention to her at all.

Lily noticed the tension in the room and how pathetic Ruby looked and she tried to chime in helpfully, "We taught Ruby how to make cookies today. They are really delicious. Do you want some, big brother?"

"No, thank you, Lily. All I want to do is spend time with my little honeybee." He started cooing to her as he took her outside.

Lily winced as she looked at her. "Sorry. He will cool down. Eventually."

Ruby threw her a weak smile as Lily excused herself to ask Iris for help on her homework. Poppy then went outside with Silver and Steve, leaving her alone with Anthony.

Ruby slumped against the loveseat, not in the mood for small talk, even with someone as sweet as Anthony. Anthony sat across from her with a gentle smile on his face. "How are you, Ruby?"

Ruby's entire body felt heavy. "Bad. It's been almost a month and Steve can barely stand to look at me. I'm afraid I have lost him for good, Anthony. He hates me, and I can't blame him. I tried giving him time, but he just seemed to grow angrier."

"I know you talked to him in the past about why you

wanted to give up the baby, but have you tried talking to him recently about it?" Anthony inquired.

"No. I don't want to make him angrier. Any mention of Silver and what I planned to do, seems to always end in tears and heartbreak. I have apologized so many times, I just don't know what else to do."

Anthony didn't speak for a while, but when he did, his voice was firm. "Steve is a proud man. All my brothers are. I have a feeling he is not just angry at you, he's angry at himself as well."

"Why should he be angry at himself?"

"Because he probably feels he has been a lousy husband. Someone you couldn't confide in when you were feeling desperate and overwhelmed enough to give up Silver." Anthony squeezed her hand. "What you were feeling at the time, the fear, is completely normal. You are a young mother who has had a very hard life. It is not surprising that you felt terribly overwhelmed and stuck in a role you did not want."

"He has not been a bad husband," Ruby whispered. "He has been more than generous. I thought being independent was what I wanted, but after Silver was born, I realized what I wanted most in this world was Steve and Silver. Now, I'm afraid it's too late. What if I lose them both, Anthony? I don't want to be married to a man who hates me."

"He doesn't hate you," Anthony said simply.

"How do you know?"

"Because if he hated you, he wouldn't be looking as if his heart were breaking every time he looks at you. Steve has had many lovers, but you, Ruby, are the only woman he has truly loved." Anthony looked at her softly. "Talk to him again, Ruby. Be open with him, sincere. Tell him all your fears without being ashamed of them. Steve will not judge you. None of us will. Both of you have to be strong and mature for Silver. You two cannot ignore each other forever."

Ruby threw him a weak smile. "I don't suppose you want to be a mediator."

He laughed. "Well, granted, marriage counseling is one of the roles of a pastor, but I think this is something you and Steve have to resolve by yourselves first."

Ruby kissed his cheek. "Thank you, Anthony, for always being so sweet. You're going to sweep one lucky girl off her feet someday."

Anthony blushed.

Ruby laughed for the first time in weeks. She felt relieved, after weeks of heartbreak. Now, it was time to get her husband back.

She found the opportunity two days later when Iris and Lily were in school and Poppy had gone upstairs to take a nap. She quickly saddled Silver into the baby carriage. Ruby didn't want to leave her alone while Poppy was sleeping, even though it was going to take longer to get into town by foot.

But she needed to do this now. The longer it took for her and Steve to mend things, the worse things would get. She needed to do as Anthony said and be completely honest with him. Ruby quickly left the house. The last thing she needed was for Poppy to realize she was missing.

"We're going to see your daddy, honey," Ruby whispered sweetly to her daughter.

Silver smiled at her in response.

Ruby grinned at her. She didn't deserve someone as sweet as Silver. She was going to try to be the best mother she could possibly be to her. Ruby would make sure of it.

Ruby had just been walking for fifteen minutes when she saw someone standing in the empty field. Clara.

The blonde stepped back, hardly believing what she was seeing. They hardly ever saw anyone in Bennington territory except for Christopher's workers. Apparently, Clara had been the exception.

"Clara," Ruby whispered softly.

She didn't know what to do. Ruby could try to outrun her, but it would be hard to do with the baby carriage, not to mention she didn't want Clara and Poppy to meet. Neither woman was the type to hold her tongue.

"I've been coming here every day, waiting for you to show up with Sara." Clara had a crazy smile on her face. "They've been keeping you under lock and key. Lucky for me, you finally showed up."

Ruby's eyes trailed towards Clara's hand, which held a large knife with an obvious pointy edge. A chill ran down her spine while Silver giggled, unaware of the fact their lives were in danger.

"Clara, please think this through. You don't have to hurt anyone."

"Oh, I think I do, you nasty, selfish little thing. We made a promise and you broke it. It's only natural I make it right."

"You sound like a crazy person."

"And you sound just like Todd. What is crazy about a mother wanting her baby? Sara is mine after all."

"She's not Sara; she's Silver!" Ruby pounced towards Clara, trying to get the knife away from her, but Clara was too fast. She managed to get away from Ruby before using her foot to kick her to the ground.

While Ruby was on the ground, Clara went to the baby carriage. When her hands touched it, Ruby screamed as she stood up, pulling Clara away by her hair so hard, she was surprised she hadn't ripped the hair from her scalp.

Clara cursed as she tried to drive the knife into her chest, but Ruby kept wiggling around. Ruby managed to grip the knife in her hand and toss it on the ground before Clara pushed her on the ground again.

Before Ruby could get up, Clara sat on her chest, her arms wrapping around her neck as she raised Ruby's head before pushing the back of her head against the ground. Ruby winced at the pain as Clara continued to smash her head against the ground until Ruby was afraid her skull would break.

Ruby managed to slap Clara across her face with enough force that caused Clara to remove her hands away from her throat. Clara shrieked as she clutched her cheek before she began punching Ruby across her once beautiful face.

Her jaw let out a small clicking sound and she was surprised she hadn't lost a tooth yet. Blood spilled down her mouth and nose and down her chin. She needed to do something; otherwise, Clara was going to kill her.

Something silver caught her eye—the knife she had taken away from Clara. Ruby managed to push herself forward until she gripped the knife in her hand. Before she lost her nerve, Ruby found herself digging the knife against Clara's shoulder and then her ankle, so she couldn't stand.

Clara screamed like a maniac when she saw the blood pour out. Apparently, she was not sensitive when it came to drawing blood, but she didn't like her own because she fainted dead away.

Ruby's entire face felt swollen and she didn't want to look at herself in the mirror. But she didn't care about her beauty as long as her baby was safe. Every inch of Ruby's body hurt, especially her face, as she crawled to Silver.

She needed to get to her. She needed to make sure her baby was safe. She wouldn't be satisfied until she saw with her own two eyes.

Ruby's head was pounding, her eyesight felt heavy, and she knew she was too young to get a heart attack, but currently, her heart tightened inside her chest. Was she dying? She felt like she was.

But she couldn't die yet, not when she was in an open

field with no one around. What if a stray animal found them?

It was very hard to keep her eyes open, the sun felt especially bright right now. She heard Silver crying in the background, but her body felt too heavy to move.

Her eyes finally became too heavy and she had no other choice but to close them. Perhaps someone would find them. Perhaps she would wake up soon and she would take herself and the baby back to the Bennington home.

The Benningtons. A few months ago, they had been complete strangers; now they felt like family. Ruby finally felt like she belonged somewhere. She wished they had spent more time together.

Eventually, everything around her became dark as Ruby felt her entire world slipping. *Steve, Silver, I'm so sorry for being so selfish in the past. I love you both.*

Chapter 17

"STEVE, you hovering over her is not going to make things easier. Now, move, unless you want me to kick you out by kicking your face."

"I just want to make sure you're doing it right."

"Might I remind you, I was the one who went to medical school. I don't tell you how to practice the law, do I?"

Ruby heard voices arguing, but she was having a hard time understanding what they were saying because everything around her was muffled. Her hearing was the least of her problems, though, because every inch of her body hurt. It felt like she had been stomped by a horse.

She opened her mouth, trying to speak, but she felt a sharp poke at her lip, then a warm sensation. Blood.

Her lips were bleeding.

"It looks bad. Should we take her to the hospital?"

"The hospital is too far, not to mention I am able to fix her, but you need to get the hell away from me. Chris! Get him the hell out!"

"No, I'm staying."

"Steve, maybe we should let Hugh work on Ruby in peace. You are a little high-strung and it might be better if you took a breather. We can wait back at the house. I'm sure Lucy can make you some tea—"

"I don't want tea," he growled. "I want my wife. The only way you are going to be able to drag me away from her, Chris, is if you fight me, and we both know I will be able to win. So, unless you want to fight me, I suggest you stay outside."

Christopher let out a loud, suffering sigh. "I did my best."

"Loads of help you are," Hugh snapped. "Look, if you two morons insist on staying here, then I need complete silence so I can concentrate."

It was Hugh, Steve, and Christopher in the room. Her husband and her two brothers-in-law. Ruby's heart jumped in her chest when Steve called her his wife. It felt like it had been a long time since he had called her that. Not to mention, it was the first time he had said it without disgust in his voice.

Wife.

It was the most beautiful word she had ever heard.

"She's crying," Christopher interrupted their squabbling. "Ruby, honey, are you okay?"

Steve practically pushed Chris out of the way as he kneeled down next to Ruby, squeezing her hand tightly. "Ruby, baby, can you hear me? Open your eyes, sugar. I want to see your beautiful green eyes."

Ruby tried doing as she was told, but she could only open them a bit. It hurt like hell if she tried to open them fully. Tears slipped down her face at the pain. "Hurt," she managed to squeak before closing her mouth.

"I know, honey." Steve caressed her face. "Don't strain yourself. Talk only if you need to. Do you want some water?"

She nodded as Steve pressed a glass against her bruised lips, swallowing it eagerly.

"Ruby, honey, what happened?" Christopher pressed.

Steve glared at him.

Chris ignored him. "We need to find out as soon as possible, since Clara is currently in the next room handcuffed to the bed."

This was news to Ruby, and her eyes widened in surprise. "She's not dead?"

Hugh shook his head. "The stab wounds didn't kill her, they just caused minor blood loss. She'll be fine in a few days. Were you trying to kill her?"

Steve tensed as he squeezed his wife's hand. "You don't have to say anything, sweetie."

"I wasn't trying to kill her," she blurted out. "She kept beating me and I just wanted to get her away from the baby." Her faced paled. "Where's the baby?"

Steve patted her back soothingly. "She's fine. I left her with the girls and Anthony. You just worry about getting better."

Ruby touched her face. "How bad is it?"

Steve tried to hide his wince. "Not bad at all. You still look beautiful."

"Don't lie to the girl," Hugh snorted. "The swelling and bruising are going to take weeks to heal, and you might have a couple of scars. They should fade over time, but you'll live. You're essentially fine, Ruby. You just need to rest for a few days and clean your wounds every day so they don't get infected."

Ruby nodded, trying not to cry. She had always been known for her beauty, and to think it might be gone, felt like too much to bear.

Christopher sensed the tension and quickly pushed Hugh out of the room, to give them much needed privacy.

Ruby buried her face in Steve's chest once they were gone and he let her sob in his chest as he patted her hair.

"Ruby, honey, what happened?"

The blonde took a deep breath and told him everything from the very beginning. Her horrible childhood, her absent parents, her dream of opening up a brothel and being an independent woman, how scared she had been to be a young mother, to the point she had accepted Clara's offer, how she bitterly regretted it, and how she had been ambushed by Clara when she attempted to go visit him to make up.

"Please give me another chance," she choked out, her eyes pleading. "I swear, I will try every day of my life to be a good wife if just you give me another chance, please, Steve."

He tucked back a piece of hair behind her ear. "I will if you give me another chance." Ruby looked confused. "I made too many assumptions, Ruby. Assumptions which hurt you. To put it bluntly, I behaved like a jackass and it wasn't fair to you. I should have listened to your concerns from the start." He kissed the backs of her knuckles. "Please forgive me, darling."

Ruby nodded, her eyes welling up with tears. When had she become so sentimental? She blamed Steve for overcoddling her. "You're forgiven. What will happen to Clara?"

His mood darkened. "She tried to attack you twice and tried to take our baby without our consent. I am sending an order to have her transferred to a woman's prison in the city."

She nodded as she rested her head on his shoulder. "She won't like it, but we'll finally feel safe."

Steve looked pleased at her answer as he pressed his thumb and index finger against her chin and raised it slightly so she was looking at him. "I promise to take care of you and Silver, Ruby, until my dying breath. You can count on it. I love you, Ruby."

With his statement, he pulled her in for a gentle kiss, careful not to hurt her, causing Ruby to melt in his arms with pleasure. She savored the kiss, feeling his warm lips on hers as he gently caressed the back of her neck.

Ruby looked up at him. "I love you, too, forever and ever."

Chapter 18

"DOES this mean you and your little wife will not be getting a divorce?" Hugh removed his cigar lazily out of his mouth. He had invited his three brothers to play cards at his bachelor home, but none of them were taking it seriously, with the exception of Christopher, who took everything seriously.

Steve placed a card down on the table. "Divorce was never an option. I wasn't going to give Ruby any way out."

Hugh snorted. "Why would you stay with a woman who didn't love you?"

Anthony elbowed him hard in the ribs. "Ignore him. He's not able to commit to a woman for more than a week."

Hugh raised an eyebrow. "And you can? When was the last time a woman went—"

"Enough." Christopher shook his head in displeasure. "We did not come here to ambush Steve about his personal life with Ruby. We are all glad everything worked out in the end."

"What will happen to Clara?" Anthony asked.

"She was transported to the women's jail today. Conveniently, Todd decided to leave the feed store to his brother and go to the city where they are housing Clara." Steve looked relieved the situation had been resolved. "Poppy will be staying with us for a few days to take care of Ruby and the baby."

Christopher raised an eyebrow. "Poppy? She's like a military sergeant. How much rest will Ruby actually get?"

"She's not too bad," Anthony argued with a frown as he protected his sister. "She did finish raising Iris and me, and she practically raised Lily by herself. Father was a wreck after Mother died."

Christopher nodded. "True. Besides, she adores Silver. She and Lily are the only ones who manage to bring out Poppy's softer side."

Steve looked at his cards. "Finn should just man up and propose to her so they can have a family of their own. It's clear they want one."

Hugh shook his head. "And get rejected for the fifth time? Even Finn has enough of a backbone not to propose again, given how many times our sweet sister has rejected him."

"Maybe she'll marry Richard," Anthony suggested hopefully. "They've been courting for a while and it's only a matter of time before they set a date at the church."

Hugh's mouth soured. "I don't want Richard Glass as a brother-in-law. He's not good enough for her."

Christopher frowned. "What, exactly, is wrong with Richard? He is a perfectly nice man."

"It's a twin thing. You wouldn't understand."

Christopher didn't appreciate his answer. "If you find anything suspicious, let me know. The last thing I want is for Poppy to marry a fool who will not be good for her in the long run."

"I'll pick you up in exactly two hours," Steve instructed her worriedly as he helped Ruby, who was clutching Silver in her arms, out of the wagon. "I'll be here waiting."

Ruby fought the urge to roll her eyes since she knew Steve was just being protective. "I know. You told me three times, Steve. You and Christopher are joining us for dinner at six."

It was two weeks before Christmas and this was the first time Steve had let her outside since the incident with Clara. She supposed she couldn't blame Steve for being nervous about leaving her alone, even if she was going to be with Lucy.

Steve looked at her sheepishly as he kissed her then landed another kiss on Silver's wiggling forehead. He watched as Ruby entered the house before he departed.

Ruby sighed in relief. She loved her husband, but he could sometimes be a bit much. She pulled out a small notebook from the pocket of her dress, hopeful Lucy would continue with the cooking lessons today.

After eating Poppy's delicious meals while she was taking care of her, Ruby was determined to become a better cook. The house was quiet when she entered, which was odd since Lucy was usually so bubbly and constantly walking up and down, knitting something, or trying to make the house as spotless as possible.

There was no trace of Christopher, either, which wasn't as odd, since he was usually outside from the very early morning.

"Lucy?"

She checked the kitchen and the sitting room, with Silver squirming in her arms. When Lucy wasn't there, she made her way upstairs even though she felt like she was invading someone's privacy.

Ruby found Lucy sleeping in the master bedroom, her

wild, brown curls spread across the pillows. There were dark circles under her eyes and she looked a bit pale. She wondered if she should steal one of Christopher's horses and run to get Hugh.

Ruby touched Lucy's arm, gently waking her. "Lucy, are you okay?"

Lucy's eyes shot open as she looked at her with confusion. A weak smile was on her face. "Ruby, I'm sorry. I forgot you were coming. I was feeling a bit tired and decided to lie down for a bit." She sat up and stroked Silver's blonde hair. "Hello, cutie, I love seeing you."

Silver gave her a toothless grin in appreciation.

Ruby still looked concerned. "You really don't look well, Lucy. Do you want me to call a doctor?"

"No, I'm fine."

"Don't be offended, but you don't look fine, you look sick."

"I vomited my breakfast this morning, so I'm feeling a little weak. Will you be a dear and prepare me some tea?"

"Of course, but I really think you should see Hugh if this continues or, at the very least, tell Christopher."

"Chris and Hugh already know. What I am going through is perfectly normal, Ruby." Lucy had a serene smile on her face. "I am to have a baby in July."

Ruby gaped. "A baby? You and Chris? Congratulations." She pulled her in for a hug.

Lucy chuckled. "Christopher and I are excited, but we haven't told many people because it is still early days. Silver will have a cousin to play with."

Ruby nodded. "I will get you your tea and then we can lie down or do whatever you feel comfortable doing."

Lucy and Ruby spent the rest of the afternoon doing just that, alternating between dozing off, playing with Silver on the bed, or Lucy asking Ruby about her pregnancy.

Before they knew it, it was six and they heard Christopher pouncing up the stairs. He opened the door, his expression softening when he saw Lucy sleeping and Silver squirming on the bed, wanting attention.

"Did she tell you?"

She nodded softly. "Congratulations."

Christopher already looked like a proud papa, which was sweet to see since he only seemed to smile when he was around his wife, his baby sister, or Silver. He was still a very serious man, but she guessed it was because he was the oldest and he had felt the responsibilities laid on his shoulders, even though most of his siblings had already reached adult age.

"Thank you, it's still early so we would appreciate it—"

"Don't worry, I won't say anything until you two are ready."

"Thank you. How was she feeling today?"

"A little tired. Her stomach has been upset. I told her to drink tea with honey. It helped me when I was expecting Silver."

He nodded. "Thank you for being with her, Ruby."

Ruby smiled as she got up from the bed and began wrapping Silver in a blanket. She suddenly felt like she was interrupting a very intimate moment between a couple. She said goodbye to Chris and headed downstairs were Steve was waiting with a confused look on his face.

"Sorry, there's no dinner," she apologized. "Lucy was feeling ill so I stayed with her to make sure she was feeling better."

Steve took the baby, who snuggled against his chest adorably. "Don't worry about it. I was starting to crave toast with butter."

Ruby giggled as she whacked him on the shoulder. "You're such a liar. Let's go home."

Once they returned to their place, Steve put the baby to

bed while Ruby quickly made some sandwiches they could dine on. Ruby sat on Steve's lap while both of them munched on their food.

Most of the bruising and swelling had left Ruby's face and it was slowly returning to normal. She only had two small scars one on her chin and one on her left cheekbone, which was a miracle in itself.

"I'm proud of you, you know," Steve announced.

"For making a sandwich?" she joked.

"No, though it was delicious." He kissed her cheek. "I'm proud of the way you have grown up. When we met a year ago, Ruby, you would have never willingly settled into domestic life nor would you have cared for anyone else other than yourself. I see how you take care of Silver and how you try to be helpful to my sisters and Lucy. What I am trying to say is you've grown a lot from the little brat who would practically shove someone if they tried to help. I'm very proud and grateful of the progress you made."

Ruby blushed prettily as she buried her face in his neck, unsure of what to say. She wasn't good at receiving compliments because she rarely got them.

Steve laughed. "Are you feeling embarrassed?"

"A little," she admitted. "You have a way with words."

"I also have a way with my mouth." He wiggled his brows. "Would you like me to show you?"

Ruby gave him a naughty look. "Please do, dear husband."

Steve's laugh rang like silver bells as he picked her up as if she weighed no more than a sack of flour even though she hadn't lost the baby weight yet, something which made her self-conscious, but that Steve didn't seem to care about. He often praised her beauty, even when she'd had her horrible, bruised face, and kissed every inch of her body as if he were worshipping a goddess.

Even when her face was healing from Clara's attack, he never mentioned it, and when she looked at herself in the mirror and was feeling particularly down, he would caress her and whisper sweet nothings into her ear while commenting that her kisses still tasted like strawberries.

Once they were in their bedroom, Ruby and Steve found themselves in a passionate embrace as they engulfed each other in kisses. Clothes came off, buttons became undone, underthings ripped between them until they were nude.

"Get on the bed," he ordered hoarsely as he looked at her beautiful, naked body.

She did as she was told, swinging her hips to make sure her ass bounced as she did so, to mock him. Steve was already rock hard, his erection red and throbbing, seeming to jump every time he simply looked at her.

Ruby lay down on the bed and her husband spread her legs as far apart as he possibly could so he was able to place himself between them.

He ran a finger down her slit which caused a shiver of excitement to go down her spine. Ruby's toes curled as she looked at him with lustful eyes.

"Do you want my mouth on your tight quim, Ruby?"

Ruby's eyes grew big as she nodded.

Steve's finger moved up and down at a more rapid speed until Ruby felt her entire body trembling with anticipation. Damn this man and his magical fingers.

"Answer me, Ruby."

"Y-yes."

"What do you want me to do?"

"Place your mouth on my quim."

"Good girl." Steve chuckled as he placed his mouth over her pussy. He ran his hot tongue down her curl-covered mound before moving on to her clit which was slowly peeking out from its hood.

Ruby clutched the pillows next to her as she felt the muscle swirl around her needy clit. Before she could come, he trailed down farther, caressing every inch of her with his tongue. He squeezed both of her bottom cheeks in his hands as he swirled his tongue against her tight rosebud.

Ruby's moans filled the room as he then parted her labia open and started fucking her with his tongue. In. Out. In. Out. Swirl.

"Steve, oh, Steve, I'm going to—"

He bit her folds gently. "Not yet, sweet cheeks, not now."

Steve gave each of her bottom cheeks a loud slap. "Get on top of me," he ordered huskily as he lay down beside her. "Ride me, my beautiful wife."

Ruby smiled at him as she positioned herself over his erection, slowly lowering herself. A groan escaped her lips. It was the first time they had become intimate since she gave birth, and it felt like she was a born-again virgin.

"Take your time," he murmured helpfully as he placed both hands on the back of each thigh to help her lower herself. "You're doing so good, sweetie."

Ruby lowered herself inch by inch, until she found herself stuffed with his cock between her legs. She had forgotten how good it felt. Ruby started riding her husband, moving her hips, her ass hitting his thighs, which only made him grow harder inside her.

Her breasts bounced in the air, slightly dripping with milk as she massaged them while she bounced on his cock, her thighs squeezing together.

Steve's entire face was flushed. He almost looked adorable as he ran his hands up and down her hips before squeezing her buttocks to push her down farther against him as he fucked her.

Ruby let out a small cry of pleasure as she felt her pussy squeeze the last bit of cum from Steve's cock as she finished riding him. His hard hand slapped her bottom with gusto, decorating it with colorful pink handprints while her fingers pinched her nipples, turning them into hard little pebbles.

The blonde tumbled down on his chest after they both finished, cuddling against her husband's neck as he wrapped his arm around her, running his hands through her sweet-smelling hair.

Her inner thighs were sticky and she ought to get cleaned up, but she was too tired to move.

"I think we made another baby, sweet pea," Steve joked as he nibbled on her ear.

She glared at him. "Don't joke about that, Silver is more than enough."

Steve didn't agree or disagree; instead, he kissed her temple. "Whatever you want, Ruby. Though I would like a little boy in the future, to teach him how to ride and throw a ball."

"You can teach Silver," Ruby corrected. Then she imagined a sweet little toddler who had Steve's black hair and cheeky smile. "A boy would be nice. Then he and Silver could play together. It can wait, however, until Silver is out of diapers. I do not need to worry about diaper changes for two children."

"Can I pick the name?" Steve rested his chin on her breast. "I don't fancy all my kids being named after colors."

Ruby rolled her eyes and punched his shoulder in response before Steve found himself between her legs again.

Chapter 19

"THANK you so much for taking care of Silver." Ruby went downstairs where she found Iris entertaining Silver with the art supplies her brothers had given her last year for her birthday. Her school bag was on the floor and a history book was open on her lap. Silver had started teething and she had become a small but adorable nightmare, hardly letting her mother sleep at night.

Ruby had begged Iris to come over after school once Steve took Lily back home because she was desperate to get some sleep, something her daughter was not going to allow easily. The January air was chilly and she was glad the holidays were over so she and her family could have a proper rest.

Iris smiled. "No problem, she's a little angel."

The little angel in question managed to drool over the colored pencils.

"You're very good with children," Ruby commented as she pulled out the cookies she'd managed not to burn earlier and gave her one.

Iris shrugged. "It's not surprising, I helped Poppy with Lily a lot when she was a baby. Besides, I have to be good with kids if I want to be a teacher."

"You're still determined to take the test in two years?"

Iris nodded, a determined look on her face. "Yes, I don't care what my brothers say or want. I want to be a teacher. It's all I have ever wanted to be since I was a little girl. I wish they could understand."

Ruby unbuttoned her blouse and then placed Silver on her breast so she could nurse. "I think they are just worried about you. The world isn't exactly made for a working woman."

"You sound just like my brothers."

"Bite your tongue. If it's any consolation, I'm glad you chose a more honorable profession. My goal was going to be to open a brothel. Your dream is much more sensible."

Iris placed a hand on her chin. "Do you sometimes miss working? If you hadn't had Silver, do you think you would still be working for Madame Eugenia?"

Ruby paused. "I do miss making my own money, though your brother is generous." She hadn't touched the money she had made during her prostitution days and decided to keep it hidden for an emergency. "I miss working, though. I must admit, even with Silver and your brother keeping me busy, I get bored at home. Perhaps when Silver is a little older. I'll convince Steve to let me get a job somewhere."

Iris snorted. "Good luck with that."

Ruby winked at her. "I can be extremely persuasive."

Iris wrinkled her nose, understanding what she was hinting at. She was still rather innocent even though she was set to graduate in two years. No doubt the influence of Poppy, who could be terribly proper.

"You do realize if you choose to continue pursuing your

teaching dream, you are giving up the chance of having a family."

Married women, and especially mothers, couldn't work as teachers once they wed. Perhaps in larger cities, it was different. But in such a small town in Wyoming, it would be nearly impossible. Iris might as well lift up her skirts in the middle of the town square.

Iris looked pained for a second as she looked at Silver. "I know, but I know for sure my dream of being a teacher is worth giving up everything else."

"Iris, you're still so young. It's all right if you change your mind."

"I won't." Iris threw her a brittle smile. "Besides, I have six siblings. I'm sure all of you will give me a dozen nieces and nephews to spoil. I've never even courted a man."

Iris was very shy and reserved—she could hardly speak to a member of the opposite sex without stuttering.

"Well, don't expect any more from me." Ruby sighed as Silver bit on her poor nipple. "Steve is going to have to be content with just one child. I don't think I can do this again."

Iris laughed.

Once they finished their cookies, Ruby hitched the wagon to the horse to take Iris home. Steve had started trusting her with the horse and wagon as long as she didn't go too fast. Iris kept her entertained as she talked about a project she was doing about George Washington.

When they got to the second Bennington home, Lily waved at them from the upstairs window. Ruby noticed she was starting to leave traces of her girlhood behind and was blossoming into a young lady.

Lily was excited about her thirteenth birthday later in the year. She already wanted to wear her hair up, wear hoop-skirts, and buy dresses which covered her ankles. Lily had even asked Christopher when she could start courting, something which had rendered the rancher speechless.

Steve had teased her by telling her when Iris and Poppy married, a fact Lily had wrinkled her nose at.

Their chatting stopped when they saw Poppy sitting outside, against the wall of the house with knees close to her chest.

Ruby cocked her head to the side. "Do you think anything is wrong? Could she be sick?" Though she doubted this, Poppy seemed to have more energy than all of them put together.

"She was feeling fine this morning when Lily and I saw her at breakfast. I don't think she's mad, either." This was a common Poppy emotion. "She looks in shock." Iris frowned. "Oh, do you think something bad happened?"

Ruby shook her head. "I don't think so. Otherwise, Steve, Anthony, or Hugh would have let us know in town." Ruby stopped the horse and Iris got out, taking the baby with her so Silver's Aunt Lily could see her.

Iris and Poppy talked briefly, but Poppy shook her away and told her to go inside with the baby. Iris still wasn't convinced something wasn't wrong, but she did as she was told.

Ruby, however, was not so easily persuaded. Instead, she stood firmly in front of Poppy. "What's wrong, Poppy?"

Poppy sighed, irritated. "Nothing is wrong. I already told Iris. I just needed a break from being in the house all day. It can be stifling."

Ruby shrugged as she sat next to her, not caring that her dress was getting dirty. "You don't usually sit outside of the house, though." Ruby paused. "You can talk to me if you want to get something off your chest. I won't tell your sisters or brothers."

Poppy didn't say anything, and for a second, Ruby thought she was ignoring her, until she reached into her dress pocket. Poppy pulled out a simple gold ring with a green stone in the center. She was holding it in the center of her palm as if it were covered in spiders.

"I got proposed to." Poppy had a dazed expression on her face. "Richard came over this morning after breakfast once the girls left. I had the most awful dress on, but he still told me I looked beautiful. Richard is like that, he always knows what to say. He can make you feel better instantly."

"Well, you two have been courting for more than six months, a proposal is not out of the ordinary," Ruby remarked carefully. She didn't know how to react, especially since Poppy wasn't acting like a blushing bride, but then again, Ruby hadn't been happy about her own engagement, either. "Are you happy about it?"

The question seemed to make Poppy wake up. A trembling smile was on her face as she looked at the ring again. "Of course, Ruby, what kind of question is that? Lucy knows this already, but before you came along, I had been courted twice, with no engagement. I just knew Richard would be the one. We have been courting for a while. He already asked Christopher for his blessing."

"Just because you two have been courting, doesn't mean you have to marry him. You could wait."

"Don't be silly, wait for what? Richard is a good, hard-working man. I will have a good life with him. I would even get to live in town near you, Anthony, and Hugh, though I will miss the ranch and being away from meddling people." She took a deep breath. "No, it's time I marry, even Christopher said so. I'm turning twenty-seven in a couple weeks and everyone already thinks I'm an old maid."

"You are not an old maid," Ruby argued firmly. "You just

haven't found a man you were fully interested in; there's nothing wrong with that. You've had a hard life, losing your parents so young. Of course, marriage was not your first priority. It's better to be alone than in an unhappy marriage just to appease society."

"Says the pretty twenty-year-old who is married with a baby," Poppy responded bitterly.

Ruby blushed. "Before Steve got me pregnant, I had no plans to marry or have children. Life changes your plans."

"But I'm different than you." Poppy's voice shook with vulnerability. "I'm not strong like you, Ruby. Besides, I want a husband and babies and a happy marriage like my parents had. Richard is willing to give them to me."

Ruby had meet Richard Glass a total of three times and found him dull. She would never see Richard Glass as anyone's idea of a dream husband.

"Oh, Pop, you'll get all of that. I just don't want you to make a choice you're not sure of because you're scared it's not going to happen." Ruby squeezed her hand. "What about Finn?"

Poppy's mood darkened. "Finn is nothing. I'm not blind, I know he loves me. Why else would he have proposed to me more than once? Even when I reject him, he still comes back like an injured dog. It's pathetic."

"Finn is sweet on you." Ruby ignored her harsh words. "He will be good to you as well. Is there any reason why you won't marry him?"

Poppy gave a long-suffering sigh. "Because he's just like my brothers. Stubborn men who believe in spanking and who want to fuss over their wives as if we were made of glass. Believe me, Finn and I would never make a proper couple. We would be too busy arguing."

"If you say so." Ruby looked doubtful.

"I do. Thank you for the conversation, Ruby. It's just what I needed to convince myself that being Mrs. Richard Glass would be the best thing that could happen to me." Poppy tucked the ring back into her pocket. "Now, be a lamb and don't say anything yet. Richard and I plan to announce it during Sunday dinner."

Chapter 20

AFTER CHURCH THE FOLLOWING SUNDAY, Steve and Ruby, along with baby Silver, made their way to Christopher and Lucy's house for the traditional Sunday dinner. Baby Silver let out a happy laugh as she clapped her tiny hands together when Steve made the horses gallop at rapid speed.

"You're going to make us fall and break our necks," Ruby scolded him.

Steve threw her a brilliant smile. "It makes Silver happy. Besides, doesn't it remind you of another rocking we do together?"

Ruby blushed. "You're such a pervert."

He grinned at her. "For someone who used to work in a brothel, you are rather uptight. And I didn't hear you complaining when I had my tongue buried between your—"

"Steve, the baby!"

Steve kissed Silver's forehead and she tried to tug on his ear.

They made it to the main house without any more squabbling. Steve had barely helped Ruby out of the wagon when Finn stormed out of the main house, a furious expression on his face.

Since Finn was practically family, he often joined them for Sunday dinners. Ruby found him pleasant and sweet, and she didn't know why Poppy had rejected him so much. Poppy stood by the doorway, an odd expression on her face, a mixture of pain and distraught.

"Is everything all right, Finn?" Ruby asked him gently. This was the first time she had seen him so angry. Hugh and Poppy were usually the ones with a temper.

Finn ignored her, turning all of his attention to Steve. "How could you let Poppy get married to Richard Glass? He's not the man for her and you know it!"

Steve barely blinked, already expecting the outburst. It was clear that while Poppy had rejected him many times, he hadn't actually expected her to marry someone else. "She's a grown woman, Finn, I can't tell her what to do. Besides, she's nearly twenty-seven years old. She should have been married a long time ago. You're just upset she isn't marrying you."

For a second, Ruby feared she was going to have to stand between the two men because Finn looked ready to pummel Steve to the ground. She didn't want to think how Finn had reacted when he had first heard the news.

But Finn would have found out sooner or later. No wonder Poppy looked so distraught. This was the first time Poppy genuinely seemed afraid of Finn. Other times, she barely looked in his direction with obvious indifference. Not now.

Finn's face turned red. He opened his mouth to argue with Steve, but then he turned away and left the ranch.

Ruby raised her eyes to look at Poppy, but she had disappeared.

Steve squeezed her arm when he saw the nervous expression on her face. "Now, don't you fret, sweet cheeks. I meant what I said. Finn and Poppy are grown adults and they have to deal with their own weird relationship by themselves."

"I just feel so bad for Finn."

"So do I, Ruby. If I'm being honest, I would prefer it if Poppy married Finn over Richard. Finn could control Poppy, but she made her choice and we have to respect it. It's high time she married anyway. Chris and I were worried she would wind up an old maid. Who knows, once Poppy marries Richard, Finn might get over his obsession with her." He frowned. "I need to talk to Christopher, to make sure the idiot doesn't steal Poppy on the day of her wedding."

"When is she getting married?" Of course, Steve and Christopher would know, Richard had probably asked both of them for her hand.

"February."

"That soon? It's only a month from now."

"Our father died in February. I think it's Pop's way of not making the month so depressing. A wedding will be good. Something cheerful after everything." Steve squeezed Silver's cheek. "This little one will be the prettiest flower girl ever. Lily is getting too old for the job. She'll be thirteen this year, old enough to be upgraded to bridesmaid."

"She'll be pleased."

Steve noticed she still looked worried because he tilted her chin so she faced him. "I mean it, don't get involved. Let Poppy deal with Finn." Ruby nodded obediently. "Let's change the topic of conversation. I never got you a birthday present. Twenty is a big birthday. Is there anything specific you want? Chocolate? A fur coat? Your own horse?"

Both she and Steve had gotten sick with colds during her actual birthday so they had not properly celebrated it.

Ruby smiled as she looked between her husband and her infant daughter. A year and a half ago, she had started working at a brothel, determined to be her own woman and sleeping with men for money, never settling down and never forming a family.

Now, she couldn't imagine a life without Steve, Silver, or the Benningtons in her life. Ruby kissed him gently on the lips, holding their daughter close between them. "I have everything I need right here."

Annabelle Marin

Annabelle Marin is a twenty-something romantic who lives in sunny California. When she isn't writing she enjoys daydreaming, watching way too much TV, and cuddling with her pets.

Her books are sweet erotic romances with domestic discipline. In her books you can expect: a spoonful of sweetness, a dash of sass, a cup of naughtiness, and an abundance of romance.

You can follow Annabelle on Facebook, Instagram, Goodreads, and Bookbub for exciting updates on upcoming books!

Facebook-https://www.facebook.com/annabelle.marin.940/
Instagram-https://www.instagram.com/
missannabellemarin/
Bookbub-//www.bookbub.com/profile/annabelle-marin
Goodreads-www.goodreads.com/author/show/21061973.
Annabelle_Marin

Don't miss these exciting titles by Annabelle Marin and Blushing Books!

Stand Alone Titles

Endless Paradise
Between Kisses & Lies
Letters to Holly

On the Dotted Line
His Southern Belle

Earthly Mates Series
The Alien's Mate

The Benningtons Series
Holy Matrimony

The Hollis Sisters Series
The Affair
The Scandal

The Stevenson Brothers Series
The Rancher Orders a Bride
The Pastor Takes a Wife
The Sheriff Finds a Fiancée

Vintage Beauties Series

Bless Her Heart
Becoming a Gibson Girl
The Modern Housewife
Vintage Beauties Collection

The Bride Series

The Unwilling Mrs.
The Unattainable Bride
The Unexpected Wife

Anthologies

12 Naughty Days of Christmas 2021

Blushing Books

Blushing Books is one of the oldest eBook publishers on the web. We've been running websites that publish spanking and BDSM related romance and erotica since 1999, and we have been selling eBooks since 2003. We hope you'll check out our hundreds of offerings at http://www.blushingbooks.com.

Blushing Books Newsletter

Please join the Blushing Books newsletter
to receive updates & special promotional offers.
You can also join by using your mobile phone:
Just text BLUSHING to 22828.